# WEST TEXAS

AN EVANS NOVEL OF THE WEST

# WEST TEXAS

AL SARRANTONIO

M. EVANS & COMPANY, INC. NEW YORK

Library of Congress Cataloging-in-Publication Data

Sarrantonio, Al.

West Texas / by Al Sarrantonio.
p. cm.—(An Evans novel of the West)
ISBN 0-87131-637-4 : 15.95
I. Title. II. Series.
PS3569.A73W47 1990
813'.54—dc20 90-24420
CIP



M. Evans and Company, Inc.
216 East 49 Street
New York, New York 10017

Manufactured in the United States of America

9 8 7 6 5 4 3 2 1

*For*
*Geo. W. Proctor*
*who*
*let me fall in love*
*with*
*West Texas*

# *Chapter One*

*Sunrise?*

Sunset. Rising on his elbows, he squinted at the orange curve of the sun at the desert horizon, dared it to burn into his retinas and harm him. He'd seen that happen once, a group of men during the war cutting a spy's eyelids off and making him stare into the sun until blinded. It wouldn't happen to him. Nothing could happen to him. The sun was darker orange, edging down away from him, afraid.

Afraid of him.

He pushed himself up further, to a sitting position, groped into the saddlebag laying next to him for his tobacco. For a moment he closed his eyes and saw shadows: the image of the sun against a bright gray sky. The merest flicker of panic went through him; he immediately opened his eyes and the world was there, in his sight.

*They will all be afraid of me.*

He laughed, thinking about God, who had formed man from mud. Wet dust. Weren't all men mud?

*And to dust you shall return.*

He thought about the man he had visited today, a year later, in one of the secret places. Dust. There were bones, but even the bones had begun to soften to the spring rains, which had been heavy this year. The secret place was too near a river bank, and he had been afraid that the bones would be gone, but they were there, the desert covering eroded away, the bones beginning to turn to dust. But they were there.

Dust.

Men were mud, mud that moved around in the light of sun, and when they died, the mud dried, the sun took the moisture and they turned to dust.

He had kicked the bones when he saw them, and some of them had turned to dust under his boot. Then he had tried to recall the man's face, and had failed, and turned to look into the sun which had been high. But it hadn't hurt him because he was not made of mud, and could not be dried. Then he ground the rest of the man to dust and left that place.

There were other secret places, and he would visit them all.

He would make new ones.

Squatting on his haunches now, he turned his attention from the sun and made himself a cigarette. He was very good at that. *Make me a cigarette,* they had all asked him at one time, in the war, because he was the best at it, with dexterous fingers that never shook or slipped, even with bad cigarette paper, or in rain, or under fire. They were all amazed at that, how he could create cigarettes with his hands.

"It's the way I am," he explained, and maybe he was looking into the sun when he said it, but they were gone when he looked back at them, and they didn't bother him then except to make cigarettes.

*Make me a cigarette.*

He made himself a cigarette now, holding a piece of the paper flat between the outer fingers of his right hand, while expertly tapping out tobacco from the pouch in his left. Just the right amount fell out. Tobacco was something the Indians had given the white man, which was why the white man was killing them off. He laughed, thinking about that, because if the Indians hadn't given the white man tobacco the white man, made of mud also, might have left the Indians alone. No, of course not; because there was corn, and scouting, which the Indians had given the white man, too.

They were all mud, Indian and white man alike, heading toward dust.

They would all be afraid of him.

This was his place, the desert. There had been other places, battlefields, and before that cities, and a house in Chicago with The Woman who he would not think about. And his mother. He almost began to cry when he thought of his mother, but even her face would not rise clearly in his mind and he looked to the sun again, but it was dropping below the horizon, running away from him.

Gone.

He smoked his cigarette, moving himself in the dust to lean back on his saddle facing east, to watch the stars rise. The air was so clear here, like nothing he had seen anywhere. It was one of the reasons he had discovered himself, coming here, away from the rest of the country and into the desert. The air, and the stars at night, were reasons he had found that men were made of mud and the sun was their enemy which took their moisture away. The fact that the sun could not hurt him only proved his infallibility, and made the sun his enemy, and made him one with the night, which robbed no one but gave the stars to all.

He watched the stars come up, rushing above the horizon to pay homage to him. He had learned their names in Chicago. There was an observatory there, and he had gone there every day, sneaking away from his mother, telling her his piano lessons went until six o'clock when they ended at four, and he had watched the astronomers get the clockwork on the telescope ready for the night and listened while they discussed what they would do. After awhile, they had come to accept him, and one of them, whose face he could no longer see but who, he remembered, had large gray eyes behind his spectacles, and large soft hands, began to explain to him what the sky was and how it worked. The man gave him a book of stars to study. Soon he had learned the constellations, and learned their workings in the sky, how they rose in groups together. And once, he had sneaked from his room and made his way to the dome at night, where the man with the large gray eyes had let him look into the telescope. And it was then that he discovered that he loved the night, and that the sun was what killed men.

Was it then?

No, later.

It didn't matter.

His mind nearly drained of thought, he watched the perfect points of Orion, marked by bright red Betelgeuse, top the eastern horizon, trailing the beautiful straight sword at his waist, centered by the glowing bud of the Orion Nebula. Suddenly fearful, he studied the eastern horizon, looking for the bright lamp of The Woman, but it was nowhere to be seen. He brought his book of stars out from his saddlebag and held it close . . .

Sound.

He knew the sounds of the desert, and this was not one of them. Far off yet; and when he put his ear close to the ground, he heard it distinctly: one man, one horse, a mile away.

He rose up on his haunches, studying the area. Nothing. It was a moonless night, as yet; Luna would not be up for a good hour and a half. Nothing to cast a shadow. But the rider was close enough to see him, if he wanted.

Quickly, he replaced the book, brought a flint from his saddlebag and drew a pile of dried brush together, lighting it. There was some dead mesquite nearby, and he added tiny sticks of it, feeding the weak fire until it built and sustained itself. More of the fragrant wood, a desert weed, and suddenly he had a small campfire, which he built until it was large enough to be seen.

Above the crackling of the wood, he listened; the sound of the stranger with the horse grew louder.

The orange glow of the fire drowned the friendly stars above, but he knew that Orion, with his ready club, would wait for him, moving slowly overhead all night.

His cigarette had gone out, and as he rolled a new one, the stranger appeared in his firelight.

"Evening," the stranger said, standing respectfully back, waiting for reaction.

Slowly, he turned his eyes from his cigarette. "Evening yourself," he said.

The other was too young. He couldn't have been more than sixteen, maybe younger. A failed beard of light brown hair dotted his cheeks and chin, and the sad, long-cultivated beginnings of a moustache, long, sparse hairs, edged his upper lip.

Too young.

"Mind if I sit?" the young man asked, nervously.

Despite his anger, he forced a neighborly smile onto his face. He knew how he must look: long overdue for a shave, four weeks in the saddle, in dire need of a bath, even if it be a dust one, his clothes unmended and dirty.

Somewhere inside, he still hoped he was wrong about the young man's age.

"Help yourself," he said, continuing to smile as the young man sat himself at a respectful distance. "You look like you lost your fellows. First ride?"

The young stranger hesitated, then smiled sheepishly. "I fell back, had some trouble with my mount. I assumed they'd wait up. We were passing through the gorge a way back, and I lost them."

He let his smile grow friendlier. "Happens to all of us. Me, I got lost on purpose, didn't like the way I was treated or the pay I was gonna get. That happens, too."

"I suppose it does."

"Smoke?" He had already taken out his tobacco, begun to roll another perfect cigarette.

"Thanks."

The young man reached out, took it from his fingers, and, as he felt contact, he knew the man was not too young after all.

"Mind if I ask your age? I've got a reason."

The young man lit his cigarette, looked up. He could tell the young man was contemplating an answer.

"Come on. I'm not your trail boss. Just interested. Came out here myself when I was seventeen."

The young man's sheepish smile returned. "You guessed it. Seventeen last month. They don't want anybody less than eighteen on the rides."

He laughed, standing up and stretching. "Don't worry about that. They've taken much younger than eighteen." He looked down benignly on the young man. "You sure you're seventeen?"

"Swear to God," the young man said. "Got a package from my mom in St. Louis, with a card in it and everything." He laughed. "Had to hide it from the other boys. Didn't want them joshing me."

"I wouldn't worry about that," he laughed. His benign look turned to one of extreme interest. "Did you know you're made of mud?"

The young man, intent on his cigarette, turned his face up; it glowed orange in the firelight. "What?"

He took a step closer to the young man, bent down. "Mud," he said, bringing the Bowie out from the back of his belt and around in a smooth arc under the young man's throat. The first pass was deep but missed the big vein, and by the time he brought the knife around again he was already pinning the young man on the ground, sitting heavily on his chest, listening to him breathe in gurgles through his neck, watching the light fade out of his eyes.

He took his time on the rest of the work, stopping now and again to feed the fire. He took most of the night. Orion with his club, with his gaseous sword, rose slowly over him and passed toward dawn before he was finished, as neat a disemboweling and skinning and cleaning as he could manage, down to the red-stained white bone. He lay the bones in the special grave he dug with the shovel from his backpack, then covered and smoothed it all over. He marked the place with his signal of rocks, making it a secret place, and then cleaned his fire up as dawn was breaking.

*Sunrise.*

"You are mud, wet dust, and to dust you shall return," he said over the hidden spot, and then he turned to the sun, watching it rise into his eyesight, daring it to dry him, pull the moisture from him as it would pull it from the bones and innards he had buried in the ground.

"I am not mud," he said, "I am God," and then he turned his eyes from the sun, tying the young man's horse behind his own saddled mount, and then he rode away from that place, ignoring the sun, looking for a place to sleep.

# *Chapter Two*

Sometimes, Thomas Mullin dreamed of the War. They were not dreams in color—were, in fact, in the bleak colors of the War itself, blue and gray. There was the blue of a sky, that much he recalled—a pale, washed-out shade that didn't look like the kind of blue sky he remembered from his boyhood in North Carolina. That was a high, clear blue, clean enough to wash in, if you could reach up that far. In these dreams, the blue was not anything you would want to wash in, was high and thin, and looked devoid of oxygen, nearly as gray as the rest of the dream. For the earth was always a sickly, bleak color, nearly gray, and the men who moved over it in ranks and lines, amidst swirling smoke, in the midst of thin cries—shouts and screams that were thin in the weakly oxygenated air—were as pale and near-gray and sickly as the earth and the weakly colored trees and the rest of the earth and sky.

In these dreams, sometimes, there were no sounds at all. There was he and his friend Ames, the man from New York City, who moved with a grim determination not to die, teeth set, eyes ahead, hands gripping his bayoneted rifle as if it encased his own soul. Mullin moved with him because he thought the man was charmed, had come through Fort Wagner and Cold Harbor unhurt while those around him had been cut down like tenpins. "They always aim for the Negroes first," Ames had told him once, "but they never hit me. Hold what you have, very tight, and it will not get away." Even then, when he had said it, there was only grim determination, no boasting, in his voice, and that determination had bound Mullin, the new boy, to the charmed man, holding himself nearby with the same hard grip Ames had on his own rifle.

"Oh, sure, that boy's been through it all," their white captain, Jeffries, graduated near the bottom of his class at West Point, had told him. "Probably hasn't even told you the half of it. They sent him to Bull Run not once but twice, and he came away without a scratch. Sent him on patrols into reb territory, he came back whole. It's like he's a ghost." He leaned closer to Mullin, winking conspiratorially. "I even heard some of his white officers didn't like the talk about him after a while and tried to get him killed. Bad for morale, having a ghost around. They figured if they sent him out alone often enough, the rebs would sooner or later catch him. They'd string him up like a chicken. But he kept coming back, slow and plodding, the way he walks, without so much as a powder burn on him. After a while they just started shuffling him around, till he got to me. But I'm not the kind to try to get him killed, and I don't believe in that charmed stuff anyway. Way I see it, nobody's charmed, not you, not me, not Ames. He just hasn't found the bullet with his name on it yet."

A week later Captain Jeffries found a Confederate bullet with his own name on it, and Mullins discovered later that Jeffries had been the one sending Ames out on patrol alone trying to get him killed, taking bets with his other white officers over when it would happen.

So Thomas Mullin stuck with Ames, and sometimes in his dreams, thirty years later, he was still with him in that pale and lifeless place that was the War, moving through thin smoke, stepping resolutely forward, around the men with bayonets in their bellies, bullets in their eyeholes, corpses left legless by cannon fire, the occasional headless man laid neatly back on the ground, still clutching his rifle . . .

"Lieutenant Mullin," someone said, and in the dream he turned to Ames, but Ames marched ever forward, never turning, moving ahead of Mullin as he left the dream behind, even as Ames left him behind, into the smoke.

"Lieutenant Mullin," someone was saying beside him, poking him roughly awake. "Lieutenant Mullin, wake up."

He came up out of sleep, rolled over, saw the blue tunic, the stripes at the shoulder of an Army Sergeant. For a moment he thought he was back in that Army, perhaps still back in that war, though the colors here were sharp and distinct, the air clean and hot, not like the thin pale lifeless air of Chattanooga—

"Lieutenant Mullin, please, get up."

He looked up into a white face. Sergeant Chase, a young man. One of the good ones. Mullin's head cleared, and he remembered why Chase wasn't saluting him.

"Yes, Sergeant, I'm awake."

"Captain Seavers would like to see you. Now, if you can manage it."

"Seavers?" he said in surprise.

"Yes, Sir."

"No need to call me sir. Not anymore, anyway."

"Whatever you say, Sir."

Mullin detected a slight smile on Chase's lips.

"Don't fool with me, boy. I can still whip your tail." He noted with satisfaction the sudden stiffening in Chase's limbs, the look of surprise on his face.

"Sir, I meant no disrespect . . ."

"Hell," Mullin said, laughing. He rose from the bed, punching at Chase's arm playfully. "I was only kidding. How are you getting along, son?"

"Very well, Sir."

"Been on patrol lately?"

"A week ago. Nothing, as usual."

"Usual doesn't mean always. I hope you remember that. Always be ready, especially for your men's sake."

"Yes, Sir."

Mullin stretched, moved toward the washstand and mirror in the corner, scratching at the white stubble on his chin. "They going to let your wife come out?"

In answer, Mullin felt Chase take his arm. "Sir . . ."

Mullin turned to the sergeant. "What is it?"

"Sorry, Sir. But Captain Seavers wants to see you right away."

"I haven't shaved, haven't washed."

"He can't order you, of course, but he requests . . ."

"That's all right, son, don't apologize. I'll come now." He pointed at his suspendered trousers laid neatly over the back of a straight chair next to the bed; on the chair itself were yellowing copies of the *Strand* magazine, pages dogeared. "All right if I wear my pants?"

Again, Chase smiled, "Of course, Sir."

Ten minutes later, Mullin was waiting uncomfortably outside Seavers' office, getting angry. It didn't feel right, him standing here in his civilian trousers, his faded red nightshirt tucked into them, unshaved, his stomach hungering for breakfast, the sleep barely out of his eyes. He felt naked out of uniform—even more so, presenting himself like this. He had been an officer, damn it, and he deserved at least to appear as a retired officer should—in clean-pressed clothes, with a good close shave and a full belly, showing respect for himself and his former livelihood. It was something he could never stand in others: slovenliness, untidiness, the appearance of sloth or inattention to details. Details were what kept a man sharp, kept him disciplined, sometimes kept him alive. They were what set him apart and made him deserving of respect. He had been an officer in an army not known for Negro officers, had fought for respect every step of the way, had deserved everything he got, and here he was, two weeks past retirement, reduced to the kind of sloppiness he had berated his men for. It was indecent, something he wouldn't stand for.

When the cook, Rivers, came out of the Captain's quarters, stopping with his tray of used breakfast dishes to stare, Mullin had had enough.

"My God, Lieutenant, is that really you?" Rivers said.

"No," Mullin snapped, getting up, marching toward the door. "It's not me at all."

Mullin walked past Rivers, opened the door, and was halfway out when he heard Seavers' voice behind him.

"Mister Mullin, please come in."

The tone of the voice made Mullin hesitate between anger and interest. If Mullin had really been rousted out of bed merely to embarrass him, Seavers' voice would not hold the hint of apology it evidenced. It was still abrupt, and condescending, as it always had been, but something had obviously happened to make Seavers treat him this way, and Mullin wanted to know what it was.

Mullin turned, letting Rivers scoot out past him into sunlight, and stared at Seavers. Despite his anger, and other feelings for the man, he had to stifle an urge to salute.

"You *asked* me to come, Captain," he said.

"Yes, I did," Seavers said. "I'm sorry if I kept you waiting. We've been very busy around here this morning, I'm afraid. Something of a crisis."

Mullin continued to stare. "Captain, I won't be demeaned . . ."

Seavers continued to surprise him, holding the door open. "Please come in," the Captain said diplomatically. "I realize how uncomfortable you must feel." Mullin didn't know if Seavers referred to his lack of clothes and a shave, or his appearance in his former Commander's office. He decided it didn't matter, accepted the gesture and crossed the room. As he passed Seavers, he once again had to stifle the compulsion to salute.

"Sit down, Mr. Mullin. Can I offer you some coffee?"

Despite Seavers' profession of a crisis atmosphere, Mullin was quick to note that the captain had not forgone either his breakfast or his extra coffee—one of the former bones of contention between the two men, since coffee had been a rather scarce commodity on the base since a Southern Pacific Railroad raid in Abilene which had appropriated almost a half ton of beans, along with much ammunition and fifteen sacks of mail from back east, earlier that year. Mullin had maintained that the coffee rationing should extend to all inhabitants of Fort Davis, officers included; Seavers had compromised by cutting the ration to his staff while refusing to limit his own intake, which he maintained he needed to help him think clearly.

"No, thank you," Mullin said, discovering that Seavers' diplomacy extended only so far, as the captain poured himself another cup.

The steaming coffee before him, Seavers settled himself behind his desk. He made a steeple with his fingers. Even now, Mullin was struck by this dandy's physical resemblance to George Custer. Seavers had gone so far as to thin his beard, darker and thicker than Custer's, so that the resemblance might be keener. Mullin had often wondered what swill they were feeding the cadets at West Point these days about the Fool of Little Big Horn; Mullin himself had gotten the story from a couple of his old friends from the Army of the Potomac, now members of Oliver Otis Howard's staff. Howard, the former West Point superintendent, head of the Freedmen's Bureau and founder of Howard University, didn't deal in myth. Custer had been a fool, and every Army man with half a mind in his head knew it, but the lesson had somehow escaped Seavers and the other officers of his kind. To obtain glory, mimic glory, seemed to be his code—a code over which Mullin and Seavers had fought for the two years since Seavers had been assigned to Fort Davis. Mullin had been deathly afraid that Seavers would enact that code in a manner which would destroy a good portion of the Buffalo Soldiers, the black command which had been sent to this Godforsaken fort in the desert of West Texas because no one else would go there. Seavers and Mullin had battled, until Seavers had finally forced him into retirement, using an obscure rule about officers that, as with many other obscure Army regulations, was either ignored until convenient, or applied more scrupulously to Negroes. Mullin's appeals had taken months, and though he was not without his champions, among them former Fort Davis Commandant Colonel Benjamin Grierson and Oliver Otis Howard himself, in the end the regulations won, and Mullin was out.

Seavers unsteepled his fingers, leaned over to drink from his cup of coffee, then leaned back again, once more making the annoying construction with his fingers. He regarded Mullin dispassionately before he spoke.

"You realize I wouldn't be asking you for anything if I had a choice," he said.

"I know," Mullin said coolly.

"The fact is," Seavers said, suddenly letting his fingers drop to his desk, "I don't have a choice. You still have some big friends back east."

For a brief moment Mullin's heart leapt—had the regulation forcing him into retirement been struck down—would he be reinstated?

"You've been asked for, specifically, to handle something, on a temporary basis, and I've been authorized to offer you a hefty bonus if you accept."

Mullin's heart sank; it had nothing to do with reinstatement. "What is it?"

Again Seavers made his steeple. "It seems a Senator's son, from Missouri, has gone and gotten himself lost in our area, in the Davis Mountains. He was out on a land scouting job with a couple of cowboys, doing it for a lark, learning about the west and all that. He managed to get himself separated from them a couple of weeks ago. They went out searching for him but found nothing. They found his horse three days later, butchered. It had been cut up like a steer, maybe for food. But there was a big sun carved in the side, and the horse's eyes had been put out. Whoever did it wasn't just hungry."

"There was no sign of the boy?"

"Nothing. These cowboys say there have been a couple of disappearances like this over the past few months, a couple of other animals, a mule, in one case, cut up the same way. None of the missing people were ever found."

"Why didn't we hear of this?"

"Apparently it's been happening far and wide. One of the cowboys had worked a ranch down near Musquiz Canyon, heard a story down there. Another one had been up North a bit, heard another story there. They just happened to be with this boy when the same thing happened."

"It could be a renegade Comanche, though I doubt it," Mullin said. "Whoever it is, the boy is dead."

Seavers' steeple dropped again. "Probably. But this is a Senator I'm talking about. He wants something done. So orders came down. I'm ordered not to spare any of my own men, because we have maneuvers out in the Eagle Mountains next week. There are . . . some rumors about Mescaleros acting up. The rest of the contingent we need here. So somebody got the idea of using you. You're to set out immediately and help the Senator's private investigators, Pinkerton men, when they get here. I'm authorized to pay you twenty dollars now, a fifty dollar bonus if you find anything. A hundred dollars if you find the boy alive."

"Forget the hundred dollars," Mullin reiterated.

"Be that as it may. Do you want to do it?"

"What happens if I don't?"

Seavers sat up straight in his chair. He had a look on his face as if this possibility hadn't occurred to him. Mullin now realized just how much pressure had been put on him. "I was hoping you would just say yes. The Army would be very appreciative."

"I'm sure," Mullin said. "Here are my conditions. The money is fine. But if I find the boy, dead or alive, I get reinstated, at my former commission, at full pay, with back pay for time lost appended."

Seavers sat up very straight; his face began to redden. "I can't authorize . . ."

"You can. The fact that you called me, when you did, the way you did, tells me you were ordered to give me anything I want. You realize, and they do too, that I'm the best man out in this desert.

The Senator must have snapped his fingers. Do you agree to my terms, Captain?"

"You cannot . . ." Seavers began, his face reddening even more.

"I have. Agreed?" Mullin held out his hand.

Seavers held the arms of his chair very tightly. For a moment Mullin was reminded of Ames, in the War, holding his rifle, and himself, holding the image of Ames. *Hold what you have, very tight, and it will not get away.* Ames had saved his life. He had been holding tight ever since.

Seavers picked a piece of paper up, held his right hand out over the desk, toward Mullin. "This has a description of the boy, including some identifying body and dental marks."

Thomas took the paper and hand in a hard grip.

"Done," Mullin said, getting up without saying good-bye, leaving the room, his back straight, heading for his room to shave and dress and pack.

As Seavers pulled his hand back, it went limp on the desk, upsetting his cup of cooling coffee, spilling it over his blotter.

# *Chapter Three*

Thomas Mullin was shaving, following the line of his jaw with a stropped razor, when the door behind him opened without ceremony. In the mirror he saw daylight obliqued by a large frame in the doorway.

"Do you always enter a man's home without knocking?" Mullin asked, continuing to shave, moving the razor expertly from Adam's apple up to chin.

"I thought . . ." the reply began.

"You didn't think," Mullin interrupted. "Sergeant Chase, who you know, and who is *white,* was in here earlier and acted in a proper manner. You think that since I'm no longer a uniformed soldier, you needn't have respect. Is that accurate?"

"No, I mean," the awkward answer came. "That is . . ."

"Sit down, Trooper Reeves," Mullin said, waving the hand holding the razor at his bed.

He watched in the mirror, smiling to himself, as the soldier did as he was told.

"You realize I can't *order* you to do anything anymore, don't you?" Mullin asked.

"Yes, I do, but . . ."

Mullin gave an exaggerated sigh, turning to face Reeves. The left side of Mullin's face was still unshaved, soap drying. "Have you been in trouble with the quartermaster again, Trooper Reeves?"

Reeves squirmed on the bed, tried to look away. "Not exactly. That is . . ."

"That's not what I heard, Trooper." Mullin turned back to his shaving, wetting the drying area with water before carefully shaving it. "I heard you had another fist-fight, and that when the quartermaster tried to break it up, you hit him, too."

Reeves was sitting very straight on the bed, eyes straight ahead.

"I also heard," Mullin continued, "that the reason the quartermaster interfered, unfairly, is that you were beating his friend Farley, and that your hitting the quartermaster was justified, if insubordinate."

In the mirror, Reeves relaxed slightly.

"Is that correct, Trooper Reeves?" Mullin said in a sharp voice.

Reeves's relaxation turned to rigidness. "Yes, it is, S . . ." he said.

Mullin turned slowly, eyebrows arching. He wanted very much to laugh, but kept his face stern. "What were you going to say, Trooper Reeves?"

"Nothing," Reeves replied, staring straight ahead. As Mullin stared at him he added immediately. "That isn't true. The word came down from Sergeant Chase that you didn't want to be called Sir. I was going to say 'Sir.'"

"I applaud your honesty. I most certainly do *not* want to be called 'Sir.' Do you understand me, Trooper Reeves?"

"Yes, S . . ." Reeves snapped, muttering to himself, "Damn."

"Was that a cuss word, Trooper Reeves?"

Reeves stopped staring straight ahead, turned to Mullin with a pleading look. "Please, let me call you Sir."

Mullin's eyes widened. He allowed a mock look of anger to cross his face. "You said 'Sir.'"

Reeves moaned. "I'm sorry, I truly am. It's just that . . ."

"I won the bet!" Mullin crowed. He grinned broadly, turned to finish the last spot of shaving. "You may call me anything you like now, Trooper Reeves. But I don't think Sergeant Adams will be very pleased with you, since he now owes me a five dollar piece."

Reeves moaned again. "*Please*, don't tell him. He'll kill me! I'm sick of latrine duty, he'll make me do it until 1900! *Please*!"

Mullin ignored Reeves's pleading, hummed to himself as he washed the soap off his face.

Finally, thinking Reeves had suffered enough, Mullin said, "That's all right, Trooper Reeves, I won't tell him. At least not yet. Why did Adams send you?"

"He didn't, Sir. I came on my own. I heard where you're going and I want to come with you."

The smile left Mullin's face. He turned, towel in hand, and regarded Reeves with real sternness. "Absolutely not."

"Respecting the retired Lieutenant's opinion, Sir," Reeves said, once again sitting ramrod straight on the bed, "I'd like to state that the retired Lieutenant will need help, and that I know the territory surrounding Fort Davis as well as . . ." he stopped, seeing Mullin's eyes narrow ". . . that is, *almost* as well as, the retired Lieutenant himself. And that, since the talk is that the retired Lieutenant will be reinstated upon successful completion of the mission, it was agreed that, and approved by Sergeant Adams, that since this objective is a desirable one to all the enlisted men, I have been authorized to offer my services to the retired Lieutenant so that the retired Lieutenant can . . ." Reeves dared to turn his head slightly to look at Mullin, smiling slightly, "became unretired."

Mullin let his anger rise, something he had never done in uniform. He dropped his towel, stepped briskly forward, and took Trooper Reeves by the ear.

"Owww!" Reeves wailed, forced to rise to his full height of six foot four, turning his head to minimize the pain in his pinched ear. "Sir . . ."

"Be quiet, Trooper!" Mullin warned, still grasping the ear, marching Reeves toward and through the door, out into the sunlight, briskly across the parade ground. Mullin walked ramrod straight, and Reeves, protesting loudly, kept up as best he could, kicking dust. A few lounging troopers, turning to look, began to laugh, but a quick stare from Mullin washed their faces to blankness. One loud guffaw sounded, and Mullin snapped his head to see Jenkins, the stablemaster, laughing loudly, horseshoe and hammer in hand outside the stables.

"Almost there, Trooper Reeves," Mullin said, forcing Reeves up the two steps to the porch of the officer's quarters. He stopped hesitating at the door, the old force of taboo reasserting itself, then took a short breath and pushed his way in, Reeves in tow.

Lieutenant Adams was brushing his moustache at his own mirror, and turned with astonishment.

Mullin let go of Reeves' ear. Reeves held the side of his head, then quickly straightened, saluting Adams.

"Sorry, Sir," he said, wincing.

Adams, recovered, smiled broadly. "Well? Did he call you 'Sir'?"

Mullin looked from Reeves to Adams. "No." He retrieved a gold coin from his pocket, tossed it to Adams who caught it deftly. "But neither is he coming with me."

Adams pocketed the coin, scratched his chin. "It's either that or latrine. And kitchen duty. And stables. You know what Jenkins thinks of Trooper Reeves, here."

Mullin took a deep breath, let his anger expand. "I don't want him with me!"

Adams, still smiling, turned to Reeves and shrugged. "Shame," he said.

Reeves said, "Oh, please!"

Mullin strode forward until he faced Adams squarely. The two men locked stares for a moment, and then Mullin said, "I appreciate it, Bill. But Captain Seavers says he can't spare anybody, and wants me to do it alone."

Adams turned his head, spit expertly into a spittoon next to his washstand. "Seavers," he said.

"That's the way it is," Mullin said. He turned, walked past the protesting Trooper Reeves and back out into sunlight.

Behind him, he heard Lieutenant Adams clear his throat, spit again.

Mullin was almost back to his cabin when Jenkins, the stablemaster, caught up to him.

"Lieutenant," he said, pulling at Mullin's sleeve, "I've got something real special for you."

Mullin looked up to see a bridled and saddled horse he had never seen before. Surprised, he said, "Where . . . ?"

"Apache," Jenkins said. "Couple of our boys found him at the base of High Lonesome yesterday. No sign of the rider. I cleaned and shoed him for you. He's a good one, Lieutenant."

Mullin eyed the horse, frowned. "I have no doubt. You said there was no sign of the rider?"

"Horse had come a little ways. Patrol checked the passes between High Lonesome and Blue Mountain. He had some wear on his hooves. Hungry, too. Don't think he was part of a war party, if that's what you're worried about. Looks like a rogue. They do get lost, Lieutenant, just like we do."

Mullin kept his frown. "Seavers said something about Mescaleros . . ."

Jenkins snorted a laugh. "This one isn't Mescalero, he's Lipan. Anyway, Seavers is always seeing Mescaleros. Wants real bad to be Custer."

Distractedly, Mullin nodded. "I suppose you're right. Thank you, Jenkins."

"My pleasure, Lieutenant. Figured you'd need a good one. Heard orders come down from the Captain about not letting any of our own go for 'civilian use.' Figured he was after your hide, make you pay." Jenkins smiled broadly. "This one hasn't been sworn into the army yet."

Mullin looked at the stablemaster, nodded his head. "I do appreciate it."

Jenkins beamed. "We all want you back, Lieutenant. Real bad."

He handed Mullin the reins, tipped his cap, turned back to the stables. "Good luck, Sir."

"Yes . . ."

Still distracted, Mullin led the horse back to his cabin, tied it up, went to pack.

# *Chapter Four*

*Cigarette.*

Expertly, he rolled tobacco in paper and put the cigarette in the corner of his mouth. He flared a bright match, covered it against the night desert breeze, lit the cigarette and dropped the match. It flared briefly, a would-be sun, but he snuffed it with his boot and it vanished. A drift of sulfur smoke reached his nostrils, but that, too, disappeared.

The stars were achingly bright tonight, a steady, untwinkling bowl from horizon to horizon. Moonless, as yet. The Milky Way had risen, a blinding white cloud ribbon from horizon to horizon. They didn't get dark skies like this in Chicago. They didn't get them anywhere.

He lay down, back against a rock, facing east, comfortable. He pulled in smoke, let it drift out of his lungs. For a moment, smoke drifted up toward the Milky Way, trailed out, joined it. A perfect mating: smoke and stars.

It would be dawn soon, and he would have to find a place to sleep. Perhaps he would sleep here, snugged into the creviced back of this rock, the rising sun covering him with shade. Shade was homage to him, the sun's frightened gift, cool acknowledgment of his power—

Abruptly, at the horizon, a brilliant point of light rose, filling him with instant dread.

As the brilliant light rose, The Woman's face rose into his mind.

He cried out, clawing at the night, the stars in front of his eyes. The Woman's face hung there, indistinct, ashen, lips barely parted, hitching whispers of breath—

"Noooooo!" he cried into the desert night, his realm. There was no echo. The Woman's face returned, hovering before him, and then the head turned, opening up to a room. The parlor. He saw the photograph, he and his mother, smiling, holding hands, he was ten, cracked and faded black and white, on the mantel. The room opened up like a fan. Piano roll music, a spring breeze billowing the lace curtains into the room. His telescope, a long hard brass tube set on slim mahogany legs, in the cusp of the bay window.

"Do you like it?" his mother's voice said. "Have you looked at the bright planet with it?" His mother's head turned to him, she held her hand out—

He heard The Woman call.

*Who was she?*

The Woman cried out again, weakly. Still, he couldn't see the face clearly in his mind. The room opened wider, fanning out; he saw the corridor, the gas lamp next to the hallway, the polished table under it holding dominoes, the deep pink chintz wallpaper. The corridor was dark, doors closed along its length. He heard her call out again, the farthest room.

"I'm coming!"

"No," his mother said. She held her hand out to stop his shoulder, but he moved under it, past her. He began to run. He entered the corridor, musty smells. There were many doors, white-painted oak, thick-framed, thick moldings around them. Heavy brass doorknobs that rattled when he turned them.

"I'm coming!"

He heard his mother behind him, calling to him to stop, and ran faster. The doors wouldn't open. He heard a key fall out of one, bent quickly down to see it under the side sill, reached his fingers through and just touched it. Long, metallically cold.

"You mustn't," he heard, and looked back to see his mother's head, bodiless, floating down the corridor toward him.

He pushed himself up, ran on.

The end of the corridor rushed up at him. He could hear The Woman breathing behind it, rattling gasps. He turned the knob, but the door was locked.

"I'm coming! I'm coming!"

"You mustn't," his mother's voice said very close, and he turned, gasping, to see her head on a level with his face, bobbing in air—

"No!"

He pushed the head away, and it bobbed back, hovering, then silently slipping toward him again.

He rattled the doorknob, heard a key drop to the floor.

He dropped to his knees, reached his fingers under the sill and closed them over the key. The Woman was fighting for breath on the other side. He stood, put the key into the lock and turned it. There was a ponderous click, and now when he turned the knob it went past the lock, and the door pushed open. He saw the edge of the bed, quilts piled high, the same breeze pushing lace curtains, a figure's bony hand raised toward him. He tried to look at the face—

"You mustn't!"

"Who is she, Mother?"

He felt arms around him, pulling him back. He squirmed around, felt his mother's, breath close and sweet, lips puckered for a kiss, her face still bodiless yet her arms were holding him, pulling him back as the door to the bedroom closed magically, the knob turned, the key engaged the lock and the corridor shrank away from him, fanning closed.

He screamed into the desert night, throwing his eyes open, away from the bright light, seeing suddenly something blocking the stars.

He sat very still. A horse.

A horse and rider.

"Who the hell are you?" he said.

The horse snorted, pawed the ground impatiently. Behind the rider, the first thin line of dawn was cracking the horizon.

The rider sat still and tall, cradling something in the crook of his right arm.

*Apache.*

He reacted as the rifle went off. The bullet tore past the thin flesh at the top of his shoulder, near the neck. He hit the horse, grabbed up at the rider, caught him, screaming, and pulled him, holding rifle and midsection, off the horse.

The Indian was startled by his quickness and strength. He was able to bring two good blows to the face before reaction set in. By then he was already on top. By light from the Milky Way, he was able to see that the Apache was older, nineteen or twenty, and he gave a whoop of joy.

By then he had the rifle up under the brave's chin, pushing down with it mightily.

In a few moments the Apache was quiet.

Scrambling, he went to his bag and drew out his knife, cursing the coming light. He worked hard, inefficiently.

In his mind, he kept the night alive, but by the time he finished the sun was up, staring at him like a baleful orange eye.

"You cannot harm me!" he screamed at it.

The Apache's horse stood nearby, docile, but when he went for it, it suddenly bolted into the morning, kicking dust, and was gone.

He thought of tracking it, but was filled with a sudden weariness. He put his knife into his bag, crawled to the far side of the rock and found the shade-giving ledge.

Already the sun had moved high, and there was barely enough shade to keep his body out of the sun.

Grunting, he pried his body under the ledge, feeling the closeness of the rock overhead. He willed his breathing to steadiness.

In a moment he had calmed. Now he felt the heat drain out of him, felt the rush in his blood slowing to a trickle.

*Sleep.*

He thought of the Apache nearby, turning to dust.

He slept, and The Woman's face did not come to his dreams.

# Chapter Five

Thomas Mullin was packed by nine o'clock. He endured a visit from Rivers, the cook, who overburdened him with jerky and beans, and an overabundance of real coffee. Thinking of Captain Seavers, Mullin accepted half the coffee with satisfaction, telling the cook to spirit the other half away for the enlisted men.

"I will, Sir," the cook said, smiling. "You pack your magazines and all that other stuff?"

"Yes, Rivers, I did."

"Good luck to you, Sir."

Mullin nodded.

The Apache horse was a good, sturdy mount. It held its saddle well and didn't complain at the weight when Thomas mounted it. Mullin was briefly reminded of the days before the Civil War, when Jefferson Davis, then Secretary of War of the United States of America, had introduced Arabian camels as pack animals to the desert of West Texas. In many ways, the experiment had been a success—but Davis' subsequent infamy had banished forever any innovations he had made.

As he passed Officers Row, with Sleeping Lion Mountain rising in front of him, Corporal Forsen, Seavers' adjutant, stepped out of the telegraph office and blocked his way. He and Forsen had never gotten along well—but neither had there been open hostility between them. Mullin had always felt that the Army stood between them—if there hadn't been the Army, Forsen, who had grown up in Virginia, and whose family had owned slaves, would have been perfectly happy with a lynching rope in his hand—or at least a horse whip. It was true that the Army, if not promoting in any sense equality, had at least demanded, out of little more than self-preservation, a kind of grudging respect. The uniform came first.

"I've had a wire I'm to pass along to you," Forsen said. Mullin was not surprised to see some of the orderly's true feelings surface, now that the uniform had been removed between them. There was no hint of the word "Sir" in Forsen's tone of voice.

"I'll be happy to hear it," Mullin said dryly.

"The Captain's gotten late word about the Pinkerton men on their way from St. Louis. They left by special train early yesterday, and should arrive in Abilene today. We expect them here by stage tomorrow night."

"Fine."

"The Captain wants me to emphasize to you that you are to keep yourself aware of their arrival, and to provide them with all assistance. When they get here, they will be the chief component of this operation, and will have full authority." Forsen looked directly at Thomas. "In other words, *boy,* when those detectives get here, you're their *nigger.*"

Thomas straightened, keeping his eyes on Forsen. From a deep, normally quiescent place, red anger boiled up, threatened to push into Mullin's extremities. The silent subject had been broached, to his face. He knew that if he let that checked anger out, he might never be able to contain it again. He gripped the reins very tightly; even the horse felt his emotion, and he steadied it, all the while keeping his stare on Forsen, who looked up at him with a stupidly defiant grin.

"I don't know if the Captain told you," Thomas said finally, his voice steady, controlled, "that the conditions of my taking this mission include a return to rank and privilege. I could dismount now and thrash your hide, but that would mean nothing. When I return, Mr. Forsen, and when I wear my uniform again, you and I will meet."

Forsen blinked, tried to continue his stare. "That's fine with me, *boy.*"

"And when we do meet, Mr. Forsen," Mullin continued quietly, reining the horse around, "you will definitely call me 'Sir.'"

He was well free of Fort Davis, up at the base of Sleeping Lion Mountain, before he looked back. He saw what he expected. There at the limits of definition, trying badly to stay out of sight, was the tall figure of Lincoln Reeves, fully loaded on horseback. Thomas wondered what excuse Adams had concocted to allow Reeves to leave the Fort, but no doubt it had been ingenious. In a small place in his heart, he thanked Adams, knowing the man had meant well.

Thomas rode on in plain sight for an hour, before climbing a slope and then dipping behind an outcropping of rock. Quickly, he dismounted, led the horse into a shallow cave and left him there, circling up over the outcropping to wait for Reeves to approach below. Leisurely, snugged into a snake-free, shaded rock slit, he had a lunch of biscuit and jerky, with a modest drink of water.

The day was hot and dry. This was what Mullin loved and detested about West Texas. A man could roast alive in the direct sun, yet walk into a covering of shade and be cool and comfortable. The air was dry as bone. Yet, even in dry season, a burst of unlikely rain could turn the trickling creeks into raging overflow rivers of flash flood. It was always hot during the day, always cold at night, a parched country that burst into life with flowers and green grass at the first hint of rain.

A kicked stone announced the arrival of Reeves's mount below. Yawning himself out of his reverie, Thomas peered over the edge of his outcropping to see the Trooper just below him, urging his horse over the rocky ground with little words of encouragement.

Mullin shook his head, smiled, leaned back into his crevice and slept for a half hour.

When Thomas mounted up again it was nearly one o'clock. The sun was passing from its overhead perch. He kept between the sun and Reeves, enjoying the other man's growing confusion.

At first, when Reeves discovered he had lost Mullin, the trooper had circled back. Mullin shook his head at the mistake, and easily avoided him. At best, Reeves's tracking ability was passable, but a few well-placed clues had easily put the young man on the wrong trail. After an hour of this foolishness, when Mullin knew he had no more time to waste in lessons, he had drawn the trooper back under the original rock outcropping, unstrapped a saddlebag and dropped it on the young man's head as he passed beneath.

"Have the feeling you've been here before, Trooper?" Mullin said.

Recovering from the blow which had crushed the top of his hat, Reeves looked up sheepishly. "Hello, Sir."

"You know, Trooper," Mullin said, leading his mount out of its restful cave and back down to meet Reeves, "I've already lectured you about calling me 'Sir.' It seems I've spent most of my time since meeting your miserable carcass lecturing you about one thing or another."

"I'm truly sorry, S . . ."

"For heaven's sake, call me Sir!" Mullin shouted. "If nothing else, it will save time. Where did you say your people were from, Reeves?"

"Massachusetts, Sir."

"And am I right in remembering that your daddy was originally from Mississippi, and made his way through the underground railroad to Massachusetts, where he immediately volunteered for Mr. Lincoln's 9th Cavalry, in which he distinguished himself mightily?"

Reeves, knowing the harsh tone of Mullin's voice and what it meant, sat ramrod straight on his horse, staring straight ahead.

"Yes, Sir."

"And did he not, out of pride in his own accomplishments, and in those of his country, name you after Mr. Lincoln?"

"He did, Sir."

"And are they all as dumb as you back in Massachusetts? Was your daddy the only brave man, and smart man, ever to come out of that state?"

"I don't know, Sir."

"You don't *know*? What *do* you know, Trooper Reeves?"

Reeves sighed. "That I am dumb, Sir."

"Well said, Trooper. And now, before I send your miserable, *dumb* carcass back to Fort Davis, with a message containing mildly scatological language for Lieutenant Adams, I will tell you what you did wrong for the past hour and a half."

At two o'clock, satisfied that Reeves was indeed on his way back to the fort, along with the message he had given him for Lieutenant Adams, Mullin got down to business. The Senator's son had last been seen near Wild Rose Pass, near Limpia Canyon, to the northeast. But the Apache horse Thomas was riding had been found to the southwest, at the far base of Sleeping Lion. Something in his gut told him to start here. He had no doubt the Senator's boy was dead, just as he had no doubt the Lipan Apache who had owned this horse was dead, too. He couldn't help but imagine a connection. No Lipan would abandon his horse, ever. The fact that the boy's horse had been found, butchered, and that this horse had not, told him that first, the Indian had been killed recently, and second, that the Lipan's horse had escaped the fate of the boy's horse. Why?

There were other reasons the death of the Lipan bothered him, too, reasons he kept at the bottom of his mind for the moment.

Sleeping Lion was not a hard mountain, but it was long and the passes were rough. He had gotten to know it intimately during Colonel Grierson's campaign against Victorio in 1880. Captain Hatch of Fort Davis had entrusted more responsibility than he had really wanted to Thomas, and, as a result Thomas had become very intimate indeed with the mountain whose outline looked like a lion in repose from the distance.

Scouting the few obvious encampments, Mullin found nothing, and decided on a more thorough examination of the far side the next day. There was a flat plateau ideal for an overnight stay just over the top, and he spent the lingering evening making his way down to it. It was a beautiful shelf of rock, giving a stunning panorama of sky and desert.

The horse began to act strangely as they broke onto the plateau. Something in its unsharp memory upset it, and it began to buck and huff nervously. Smartly, Thomas dismounted, taking the horse by its bridle, and sought to calm it down.

"Whoa, you take it easy now," he said, pulling the rein close, making the horse look him in the eye. "You just stay with me and everything's fine."

Walking slowly, he led the horse on the plain.

There was nothing obviously wrong. The sun had moved toward twilight, shadowing things more darkly than Thomas would have liked, but the area looked as he remembered it, a rocky meadow, short grass and boulders, a few low cactus bloomed to yellow roses. The copperheads and rattlers by and large didn't like the mountain height, but there were always scorpions to think about.

Still, Thomas found the hairs on the back of his head rise.

The horse snorted, kicked back, nearly made Mullin lose hold. He calmed it, jumped as a lizard smaller than the width of his boot scooted across his path.

"Just a lizard, boy."

He moved forward carefully, cursing the setting sun for robbing him of full sight.

He felt it before he found it, snugged into the base of a chest-high boulder with a slit cut out of its base on the western side. A brush of dirt, the light prints of an unshod horse in agitation, torn buffalo grass.

He patted the horse, soothed it, tied it to a nearby stunted cottonwood.

"What have we here," he said to himself. The chill had passed from him, and he was all cold detachment now. He got down on his hands and knees, pushed the buffalo grass gently aside, was surprised to find the entire clump come away from the ground, free. It had been ripped up, replaced to cover a disturbed area.

The horse winnied, stomped behind him.

"Just stay steady, boy," Thomas said.

An area approximately six foot round had been dug up, filled in, covered. It was a good job. Mullin had no doubt that the grass cover would eventually have blown away, but by that time it might have rained, and, before long, new, sturdy ground cover would have replaced it. He was only able to determine the area of the filled in area itself by careful examination, it had been so carefully refilled and brushed. It was eerily artist-like, the way the ground had been artificially leveled, then brushed out way beyond the limits of the hole to conform with the color of the existing topsoil.

Thomas returned to the horse to remove a foldable Army shovel from a saddlebag, then returning to the spot to dig.

He had imagined a shallow impression, but was wrong. After a half hour of hard digging, during which the sun pulled down even farther away from him, he had produced nothing. He decided to concentrate on the middle of the hole, pushing deep thrusts down and pulling earth out to a depth of three feet, but still finding nothing. He was about to give up, at least for the night, when an odd thought struck him, and he angled out to the perimeter of the hole, digging there.

Almost immediately, he uncovered a nearly stripped bone, resembling a human forearm.

He moved along the perimeter of the hole, digging down, and soon uncovered other body parts: leg bones, fingers, a rib cage hung with ragged strips of flesh. The light was failing, but, at the western edge of the circle he had made, he discovered that the hole edged out from the perimeter. When he dug there he found, buried just below the surface, a cross of stones and, just below it, a human skull, long strands of hair still adhering to the mostly torn away scalp at the top. The skull, eyes facing west, was filled with the body's rotting innards.

Thomas examined his find dispassionately until his light began to fail as the sun lipped the horizon.

Mullin abandoned his find, carefully unpacked his roll from the horse and built a fire. There was just enough light to gather dry grass and branches from nearby junipers. The stunted cottonwood the horse was tethered to had a few dead branches at its top, and he broke them off.

The fire started small in the thinly oxygenated air, but built from smoke to weak light until Thomas added the larger branches, which provided some warmth and better illumination. The sun was gone now, and a peppering of stars, bathed in zodiacal light, broke the deepening blackness.

Thomas meticulously readied the rest of his camp, unrolling his bedroll near the fire side of his dig, and bringing out his Army canteen. He opened a can of beans, preferring to eat them cold, finding a rock for a backrest. He ate slowly, thinking about what he had found and what it meant.

A sound stiffened him. He had been so immersed in his thoughts that whoever it was had gotten very close, nearly right behind him. Cursing to himself, he eyed his rifle, still slung on the saddle. The horse was about twenty feet away, too far to run.

There was the merest trace of sound, behind and to his right. Thomas tossed the can of beans to his left, ducked and came around in a crouch, facing the attacker.

"S . . . Sir?" Lincoln Reeves stammered, eyes wide at Thomas's ready anger.

"Trooper! What in hell . . ."

Reeves now stood at attention. "I'm sorry, Sir, but I have my orders. I was told to follow at all costs, and to aid in whatever . . ."

"That's enough! How in hell . . ."

The merest trace of smile crossed Reeves's lips. "I've been following you all afternoon, Sir. Seems you did teach me a thing or two. I even remembered to leave my mount about a half mile back, so that its noise wouldn't alert you."

Some of Thomas's anger released. He nodded, scratching his cheek. "Have you eaten, Trooper?"

"No, Sir. Been too busy being quiet to eat."

Mullin took three steps, recovering his can of beans. He sat down with his back against the rock, leaving room for Reeves. "Well bring your damn horse up here then, and eat."

"Yes, Sir!" Reeves said smartly, saluting, then stumbled back into the darkness to find his mount.

"Can I ask you something, Sir?" Reeves asked later. They were in their bedrolls, as close to the fire as they could get. Mullin had dug a pile of *Strand* magazines out of his pack, and lay up on one elbow, pages turned toward the fire, reading.

"Hmm?" Mullin said, turning his eyes from the page toward the young man.

"Well," Reeves began tentatively, "me and some of the fellas, we've been wondering why you read those things. Charlie Hamilton, he heard you spend half your pay on those magazines."

"Not half, Trooper. But they do cost a bit. I have them sent from a place in New York that gets them right from London." Muliin went back to looking at the page he had been studying, a story illustrated with a lithograph of a tall, straight-backed man with one arm draped across the top of a mantle. "Ever hear of Sherlock Holmes, Trooper?"

Reeves shook his head.

"He solves crimes. He's a detective who uses his head. He sees what there is to see, and the clues tell him all he needs to know."

"Is he good?"

"He's real good, Trooper. I found one of his stories by mistake a few years ago, in *The Presidio County News*, of all places. Lieutenant Adams told me they were written by a man named Conan Doyle, and that they came out in The *Strand* magazine. Well, I took to that story so hard I just had to see those stories when they came out, so I found a man through an advertisement who could send me them so I could keep up with Sherlock Holmes." Mullin eyed Reeves, lifted a *Strand* and held it out. "Want to try one?"

"Thanks, no," Reeves said, embarrassed. "That Sherlock Holmes sounds real interesting, but I can't read too well."

Mullin's look leveled. "Can you read at all, Trooper?"

"No, Sir."

Mullin sighed heavily, rose up to a sitting position. "I taught myself to read when I was twenty years old. It's been the best friend I ever had. There was a man named Ames in the Civil War who told me to learn, and I told him no, I couldn't do that. He made me start. I kicked and screamed about it, but pretty soon I caught on, and nobody could stop me after that." Mullin scratched his cheek. "Now, are you going to kick and scream?"

Reeves held up his hands. "Sir, I don't think I could do that . . ."

"Why don't I read you one of these stories. You see if you like it. If you do, we'll take it from there. Agreed?"

"All right," Reeves said.

Mullin dug through his pile of *Strand* magazines, found a particular issue. He folded the pages back, angled the magazine toward the light and began to read.

"The Adventure of the Copper Beeches . . ."

When Thomas has finished, he looked up. Lincoln Reeves was spellbound. "That's the same look I had on my face the first time I heard about Sherlock Holmes."

"That sure proved Charlie Hamilton wrong. He said you crawled around looking at hoofprints and studying things because you got dinged on the head during the War."

"Did he?"

"Sorry, Sir," Reeves said. "It's just that, you see . . ."

"I see fine," Mullin said.

"Please don't hold it against Charlie. He talks a lot . . ."

"He's not the only one, Trooper." Mullin put the *Strand* magazine back in the pile, prepared to lay down and sleep.

"Sir?"

"What is it, Trooper Reeves?"

"Do you really think people as bad as that Mr. Rucastle in that story exist? Do you think people who do things as bad as that exist?"

Thomas threw his bedroll off, and got up. "Come with me," he said.

Puzzled, Reeves got up and followed Thomas to the dug-out spot by the boulder.

"That's where the skull is," Thomas said, pointing to the shallow cross at the western edge of the circle. "The rest of the bones are laid around below it."

"Is that the boy we're looking for?" Reeves said in amazement.

"No," Thomas said quietly, "this is the Lipan Apache whose horse I'm riding. But when we find the Senator's son this is exactly what he'll look like."

# Chapter Six

The Pinkerton Men were used to train rides. But only one of the four had been on a stagecoach, and that had been when he was sixteen, growing up in Wyoming before moving to St. Louis. His name was Porter, and though his butt was as sore as the rest he wouldn't admit it.

"You're just tenderfoots, boys," he boasted, feeling, for some reason, that all this land west of the Mississippi belonged, at least among this group, to him. It was also a way to get on Murphy, their leader.

"You okay, Captain?" Porter asked, his voice just a bit too solicitous. "You'd like me to ask the driver to slow it down a little? Maybe I could get you a cushion?"

"Shut the hell up, Porter," Murphy snapped. The other two, Sommers and Chaney, were slumped in their corners of the coach, looking sick.

Porter hooted, looked out the jarring window at the dimly rising mountains in the hazy distance.

"Where the hell are we, anyway?" Murphy said. "Climb up and ask the driver."

"Don't have to," Porter answered. "I'll wager those are the Davis

Mountains. Only ones they could be. I'd say we have another half day. Any luck, we'll be at the fort by nightfall."

"Darkies," Chaney said, raising his head woozily to glance out the window before laying it back again.

"That's right," Porter said. "Whole fort full of 'em. Can't believe they get anything done. Then again, this is the middle of nowhere, and, from what I hear, since they killed off Victorio, there ain't nothing to do. Sanders at the office told me he heard through the grapevine Washington is thinking of closing Fort Davis down anyway, since the two rail lines don't go near it. He laughed. "Can't see any use in paying darkies if there's no crap to shovel, know what I mean?"

Sommers had risen painfully from his corner and glared at Porter balefully. "That's enough," he said.

The coach hit a stone, bouncing hard, and Sommers groaned.

Porter grinned, enjoying the bounce. "What's eating you, Sommers? Got a little cocoa blood in you back in the dim past?"

Sommers tried to glare, held his stomach instead.

"Abolitionist," Chaney said weakly, not raising his head. "From way back. His father ran the underground in Lexington. Ain't that right, Sam?"

Sommers nodded weakly, groaned.

"Well, " Porter said, "I still say it's more than that. Never can tell, hey, Sam? Too bad they popped Lincoln, or we'd all be *sleeping* with 'em!"

"I said that's enough!" Murphy said.

"Well," Porter said sullenly, "leastways, we know this darkie Mullin they sent out after Senator Loggins's son will take the fall if we mess up, right? Wasn't that the whole idea? I mean, ten to one the kid's dead, between the heat and the mountain lions. From what the senator's secretary said, even Loggins seems to understand that. So why the big show, except to make Fort Davis look bad? This way, when they close the Fort, they got an excuse to disband all those darkies, right?"

Murphy's face was flushed red. Momentarily, he had lost his

queasiness, and raised his hand as if to strike Porter.

"If you ever open your mouth like that again," Murphy hissed, "I'll make sure you're back in that St. Louis warehouse I found you in, getting drunk and guarding crates. You're not paid to think, you're paid to do what I say. Understand?"

Porter cowered for a moment, then smiled slyly. "Sure, Captain. Whatever you say. And, speaking of drinks . . ." He reached into his hip pocket, produced a flask, watched Murphy's gaze follow it. "'Bout that time of day, wouldn't you say, Captain?"

Murphy grit his teeth, and didn't take his eyes off the flask. "How long we got before we get to the Fort?"

"Hours, Cap. Six, at least."

"Well, all right," Murphy said, already reaching for the flask as Porter, smiling, offered it.

# *Chapter Seven*

"The thing that bothers me," Thomas said the next morning, as they broke camp, "is what that Lipan was doing out here alone." He joined Trooper Reeves, who stood studying the circle of bones in morning light. It was cool and clear, and before Thomas joined the young soldier in studying the Indian's remains he let his eyes roam over the newly shadowed mountains pushing away the mist, wreathed in blue morning illumination. The beauty of this country, as obvious as its harshness, was something he never wanted to get used to.

"Gonna be hot later," Reeves said, pragmatically.

"Yes," Thomas answered. "But did you ever notice . . ."

"Lieutenant?" Reeves interrupted.

Mullin squatted down beside the trooper, who was scratching at a portion of the dug-out circle. "What is it?"

Reeves had uncovered something, a circlet of beads, and held it up for Mullin's inspection. "I may be wrong, Sir," Reeves said, "But this isn't a Lipan Apache."

"Mescalero," Mullin said. "That's what I was afraid of."

"What would he be doing here?"

"Scouting. There's probably a couple of hundred somewhere west of here, waiting for him to return. They figured that with Lipan markings, on a Lipan mount, nobody would question him. The Lipan don't bother anyone. The Mescaleros . . ."

"What's going on, Lieutenant?"

Thomas regarded the young man solemnly. "You weren't here for the war with Victorio, were you?"

"I came in right after it. I would have gone on the next campaign."

Thomas nodded. "We made a lot of enemies. Some of them hid safely across the Rio Grande, some of them went sullenly back to their reservations in New Mexico. For a while, we patrolled through Big Bend, down around the border. But that was expensive, and Washington called it off. We killed Victorio, but he had a lot of relatives who vowed vengeance. If I had to guess, I'd say we were dealing with an old chief named Pretorio, Victorio's brother. I had a run-in myself with him." Thomas stood up, stretched his back. "I imagine Pretorio figures it's time."

"Time for what?"

Mullin stood thinking, turned to Reeves. "You're going to have to go back to the fort."

"But Sir . . ."

"You're going to be my Dr. Watson. I want you to do two things. First, go to Adams, and get him to go with you to Captain Seavers. This is no jest. It'll take that fool Seavers two or three days to screw up the courage to do what he has to do. Tell Adams to look west of Fort Davis. They may still be in the Eagle Mountains. If it's Pretorio, he wants the fort badly. Tell Seavers not to send too big a patrol out, and to keep the fort well-protected. If they get at the fort it will fill them with blood, and the Lipans just might join them. Then we'd have a full-scale Indian war on our hands. They could kill a lot of people before we stop them."

Reeves wanted to ask questions, but the look in Mullin's eyes made him stand straight and salute.

"Yes, Sir," he said.

"I'll spend today here, then head up to Limpia Canyon. I'll be looking for the boy. The second thing I want you to do is get into the records, check the newspaper files, use the telegraph to check Marfa and Alpine, for any disappearances in the last couple of years. Anything. Army deserters, missing herdsmen, settlers, anything along the lines of the missing boy. Come back with the Pinkertons, if you can, and with the information." He took Reeves by the shoulder and squeezed it. "And Trooper . . ."

"Sir?"

"Be careful. There's something dangerous out here, in the mountains, the thing that killed this Mescalero scout, and I don't like it at all. Avoid contact with *anybody* on your way back to Fort Davis. If you see someone, mark the position, get as close as you can to make a description, and keep going. You hear me?"

Reeves mounted his horse. "I hear you, Sir."

Mullin gave a slight smile. "Be as quiet as you were sneaking up on me yesterday."

Reeves smiled back, reined the horse around.

"Thank you, Sir."

"Go on."

Frowning, Mullin watched Reeves pick his way off the plateau down and out of sight. Then, his frown deepening, he turned to study more closely the circle of remains.

# *Chapter Eight*

From the black shade of the shallow cave in the sheer eastern face of Blue Mountain, he watched the rider make his way down Sleeping Lion Mountain in the lengthening shadows.

*The Sun is running from me.*

*Yes.*

He thought of the sun, dropping behind Blue Mountain behind him, putting a half mile of rock between him and itself. It was good that the sun did that; he felt that soon he and the sun might have their final battle, the Battle for All of the World, and he wanted the sun to rest, to be ready, because if he defeated it in its full strength, there would be no question about his supremacy.

*Rest, Sun.*

*And die.*

He stretched, angling himself up against the mouth of the cave, then squatted, keeping his eyes on the rider below. He had spotted the horse an hour before, on wakening, and had taken it as a good omen. He knew that there would be much killing before the Battle for All of the World—as, indeed, there would be much killing after—and he wondered if this rider was one of the Sun's army, sent to kill him so that the coward Sun could avoid the inevitable battle.

*Yes. He must be part of the Army of the Sun.*

He knew now because of the glint of sunlight from the man's rifle, his erect bearing, his air of authority.

*Make me a cigarette.*

He had seen these riders before, the Army of the Sun, patrolling the hills and mountains together. He never came close to them. Usually they rode in packs. At first a thrill of fear had coursed through him, knowing that he had become powerful enough that the Sun would bring its army to bear against him. In the beginning, he had been fearful that they might prevail against him. But he stayed well clear of them, watching from a distance, and they had never come close to his hiding spots, had only roamed the hills and mountains like ants and then crept home to their camp on the far side of Sleeping Lion Mountain. He had gone close enough to see their camp once, and had gasped at its magnificence—a tiny city, a tiny Chicago of buildings with wood smoke and a flag. For a moment something had seized him, seeing that flag, and, uncontrollably, he had stood at attention, right hand raised to his forehead in salute, before bringing himself under control and realizing what had happened. The Sun had fooled him once into joining its army, but he had left, and the Sun would never fool him again.

*Make me a cigarette,* they had told him—but no one would ever tell him to make a cigarette again.

So he lowered his hand from salute, and ran from that place, back into the sanctum of the cool mountains, away from the Sun, seeking the dark, knowing that the Sun was a cruel enemy who would fool him if it could, and would do anything to defeat him.

And, eventually, he had grown to realize that the Army of the Sun could not find him, only flounder in the desert and the hills and mountains, and as long as he stayed well away from them, they would not catch him.

But this rider was different, he felt. For the first time, he saw one of them alone, and this troubled him. Why did they no longer travel in packs? Was it because they had gained strength? Or rather was it because they were vanquished already, their tiny Chicago abandoned, the Army of the Sun routed, running, even as the Sun ran from him now, behind this mountain, cowards . . .

Another horrible thought struck him.

*No.*

Eyes wild, he traced the route of the rider back from his headed course toward Limpia Canyon into the crooked trails of Sleeping Lion Mountain. It was inconceivable.

*No.*

Gasping with anger, he climbed like a spider out onto the thin ledge outside the cave, mounted his horse, and began to make his way into the ravine below.

By the time he reached it an hour later, the sun was down and a few weak stars were up. There were clouds, thin, high, a bad omen. He was moaning softly to himself as he made his way to the spot, four miles away, where the rider had reached the foot of Sleeping Lion Mountain.

When he reached it, the night was completely clouded over, and far away, silent flashes of lightning illuminated the sky at the horizon.

*No.*

Energy pumping through him, he rode up the mountain, following the trail of the soldier's horse, picking his way through the dark. A thunderstorm was approaching. He could feel its coming tingle on his skin, watch the rising banks of clouds over the top of the mountain before him.

Late in the night, he reached the top, kept moving down the other side toward his destination. The first splatters of fat rain hit his back, but he ignored them; ignored the first slaps of thunder and lightning, which only briefly lit his scrambling route.

He reached it near dawn.

He was soaked to the skin, shivering. He dismounted and stood on the edge of the plateau, unbelieving, as lightning flashed overhead, opening the sky with sound and a booming hail of frozen rain.

"*No!*"

He threw his hands to his head, closed his eyes, willing the scene before him to change, to go away, to transform away from the sacrilege he saw.

A hollow boom of thunder; a zig-zag of blue lightning struck the side of the mountain to his left, starting a hissing fire in the dry grass covered now with cold hailstones.

*"No!"*

He ran forward, dropped to his knees. Still he could not believe what he beheld.

He fell forward, raked at the open circle with his hands, began to cover the naked bones, the staring stripped skull in the hollow at the circle's head.

*"You cannot do this!"*

He kicked dirt into the circle, graded it with his thrashing body, dug his cold hands into soil, pushing away hailstones, seeking to make the horror he saw disappear.

*"I'll kill you all!"*

Impulsively, he turned, drew his knife, cut his horse's throat.

The thunderstorm drew away, left breaking clouds and a coming morning.

The sun peeked up through a lip of lightening clouds, in the east.

Enraged, he stood tall on the edge of the plateau, faced the sun full and held his open hands out toward it, gripping them closed.

The sun opened high above the horizon, scattered the clouds before it like a shepherd, drew day to itself and stared, a silent, burning eye, into his face.

"I'll—kill—you—all!" he screamed, staring straight into the sun, frozen, daring it to go back down below the horizon, banished beneath his power.

Eyes open, he stared into the baleful eye as it rose higher and higher.

The day went on, and sometime in its midst, when the sun was high overhead, as he stood still, head thrown back to stare into it, he went blind.

# *Chapter Nine*

Lincoln Reeves took an instant dislike to the Pinkerton men. Maybe their attitude was bad because they hadn't slept long enough after their trip. They had come in the night before, and from the looks of them, including their Captain, Murphy, they had not gone right to bed. Adams said there had been a poker game in the officer's quarters, and a lot of drinking. Adams himself had gone to bed at three, just as a tremendous hail storm dropped nearly an inch of ice on the parade grounds, making sleep impossible for everyone.

There was coffee in a silver pot on Seavers' desk, but the Captain didn't offer any to Private Reeves. The Pinkerton men and Captain Seavers all had cups in front of them, and the remains of a hearty breakfast were scattered around the Captain's office.

"Would you tell these gentlemen what you told me, Trooper Reeves?" Captain Seavers said.

Reeves stood at attention. "Yes, Sir. Lieutenant Mullin . . ."

"*Mister* Mullin," Seavers corrected.

"Yes, Sir. Mister Mullin found the body of the dead Indian whose horse was brought in, and discovered that it was a Mescalero in the disguise of a Lipan Apache. Lieutenant . . . Mister Mullin believes that this Indian was an advance scout for a group of renegade Mescaleros, probably camped somewhere west of Fort Davis, possibly in the Eagle Mountains, and that a contingent should be sent out immediately to intercept this force. He also believes that this advance scout was butchered by the same person who butchered the Senator's son's horse, and may have killed the Senator's son. He is presently on his way to the area where the butchered horse was found, near Limpia Canyon, where he will search for the Senator's son."

"Wasn't there more, Trooper?" Seavers said.

Reeves, who had begun to relax, snapped back to attention, stared straight ahead. "Sir. Also, Mister Mullin would like me to check, by telegraph and file, the surrounding area for similar disappearances over the past two years."

"You mean this Mullin thinks there's a crazy person out in the desert, murdering people?" Murphy said, incredulously. For the first time since Reeves had walked into the room, the Pinkerton party's head showed signs of being awake.

Porter, who had been sitting in one corner, eyeing Reeves, guffawed. "Like Jack the Ripper?"

Seavers looked at Reeves. "Well?"

"I wouldn't know about that, Sir. I only know what Lieuten—what Mister Reeves told me."

"Preposterous," Murphy said. He leaned forward in his chair, gave his attention exclusively to Seavers. "And if you follow me, Captain Seavers, I think the Senator would not like to hear that his son was just one of many victims of a madman who had been roaming the mountains in this area for God knows how long. You'll forgive me for speaking bluntly," he continued, "but I don't think this is an area we'd like to pursue. What I'd like to do is spend the rest of today getting provisions together, and then set out early tomorrow morning—say, about nine o'clock, and meet up with this Mister Mullin in Limpia Canyon. We came here to find the boy, and that's all we're going to worry about. Perhaps Trooper Reeves here," he continued, briefly acknowledging Reeves' presence, "could take us there. Would that be all right with you, Captain?"

"Certainly," Captain Seavers said. He steepled his fingers, turned a cool eye on Reeves. "Do you understand what was said here, Trooper? Do you understand that you are to be at these men's disposal tomorrow morning, and take them directly to Mister Mullin?"

"Yes, Sir."

Seavers' tone hardened. "And do you realize that whatever you spoke about some madman running around the Davis Mountains killing people is not to be repeated?"

"But Sir . . ."

"And that," Seavers continued, nearly shouting, "I don't want to hear another word about it, or hear a breathed word about the possibility?"

Reeves stood straight and tall. "Yes, Sir. But may I ask, Sir, if the Captain understands the urgency with which Mister Mullin placed on the fact that the Indian body he found was Mescalero?"

"I'll deal with it in my own fashion, dammit!" Seavers shouted. Then his voice dropped to curt dismissal. "Get out," he said.

Reeves saluted, turned smartly, and walked to the door. As he opened it and went through he heard one of the Pinkerton men, Porter, the one who had guffawed, it sounded like, say, loud enough for him to hear, "Stupid darkie."

Adams, who had waited outside Seavers' office, joined Reeves immediately. "I heard the yelling," he said.

Reeves was tight-lipped. "Did you hear everything, Sir?"

"No. What happened?"

"Nothing, Sir." Reeves fought to control himself, balling his fists at his sides, while Adams looked on, perplexed.

"Reeves?"

Reeves took a deep breath, looked into Adams's sincerely concerned face, and relaxed. "It's all right, Sir," he said.

"It's nothing."

"Well," said Adams, "I heard enough. I don't want you to worry. I'll do the checking Mullin wanted myself. I'll have whatever I can for you tomorrow, before you leave. You can take it back to him, like he wanted. All right?"

Reeves smiled slightly, nodded. "All right, Sir."

"There's ways to beat the bastards, right Reeves?"

Reeves nodded again, and his smile became wider.

"Yes, Sir, maybe there are."

# Chapter Ten

In the midst of the hailstorm, as Thomas found shelter in a tall rock overhang at the far base of Sleeping Lion Mountain, he heard the eeriest sound he had ever heard.

It was not identifiable, which made it all the more eerie. It wasn't a mountain lion, or a cow in heat, or a hurt deer or antelope. It was a bit like all of these sounds, with all of the naturalness removed, leaving only the ethereal. Coming out of the hailstorm, out of the bizarre lightning flashes amidst a rain of ice stones, out of the booming thunder banging off the mountains, it sounded like the wail of an angel—or devil. A high, pained, faraway screech of pain, it sounded like the storm had ripped a hole in heaven itself to let the cry of an agonized creature through.

Despite his hardness, Thomas felt a trail of cold crawl up his spine to the back of his neck. A shiver ran through him. The cry came again, a long, mournful, pained wail, and then suddenly it ended—and with it, the storm. Morning had come. The clouds blew themselves away, leaving the ground covered with a cold mist produced by melting hailstones, and the sky the fading memory of hell.

That was it—a memory of hell.

Thomas remembered now the Baptist preacher who had come through his home town in North Carolina once. There had been a tent meeting, something that happened only once every couple of years, and everyone from the surrounding towns was there for it. It had been mid-August, hot and humid, with horseflies as big as the round of Thomas's thumb buzzing around the lanterns and up to the top of the tent.

The preacher had started at dusk, and railed half the night about the horrors of hell and the salvation that awaited those—and only those—who availed themselves of Jesus. There had been much confession of wickedness, and some singing, but the part of the show that had impressed young Thomas most was the preacher's vivid description of hell. It was a place, slate gray, where the sun never shown but where it was always felt. Where the wicked would roast continually, right out in the open, and not a step could be taken without the fires of God's condemnation burning the soles of the feet. The sky roiled in red-gray sulpherous clouds, and the wailing of the justly punished filled the air continuously. And there had been something else, which Thomas could not quite remember, that had set him hiding his face, burying it in his grandmother's breast . . .

Years later, during the War, Thomas had remembered that preacher and his description of hell, because, visually, it had been just like that in Petersburg, and Fort Pillow. Only, the sounds of the dying on the battlefield did not quite match the preacher's vivid descriptions. Dying men sounded like dying men, and the wails of the wicked did not fit with the sulpherous smoke of cannon and rifle fire, the blue-gray of the skies, the fog of morning mingled with the pictures of death and marching men.

But, now, Thomas had something to fit the preacher's sound.

The morning cleared. Thomas listened for the sound again, but it did not come. It had faded away along with the nightmarish storm and the night. By the time Mullin had checked his horse's saddle, pulled a length of jerky out to chew on while riding, and mounted, the day was as lovely as any day in the Davis Mountains.

As he urged the horse gently forward, he heard a distant sound in the new morning, a thin wail, but it was only the cry of a coyote to its mate.

Thomas rode all morning, with a nagging feeling in the back of his head that he should be looking for something. There was very little between where he was and Limpia Canyon, and yet the remembrance of the shallow grave he had uncovered the day before, and the way it had been set, gnawed at him and made him sure that there was something he could do to help his investigation while he rode. But it wouldn't rise into his mind. Instead, he could think of nothing but Sherlock Holmes.

*I wonder how my Watson is doing.*

He thought of Trooper Reeves as he caught sight of a turkey buzzard circling high overhead, languidly waiting for prey.

That night, camping near the opening to Wild Rose Pass, he made a bright fire and was unable to sleep. Thoughts of the night before, the storm, the eerie wailing, would not leave him. The new night was clear as a bell, as far from the previous evening as possible. But in his mind, he still heard that wailing. Again, something pressed at the back of his mind, would not come forward.

Angry with himself, the failure of his discipline, he banished all thought, pulled the *Strand* magazines from his pack and moved closer to the fire to read. Opening to the first page of the first magazine, he gave a start of recognition, felt the thoughts that had been bothering him all day long shoot to the front of his mind.

*The Hound of the Baskervilles, Part One,* read the Sherlock Holmes tale, complete with a horrifying woodcut of a vicious beast, barely recognizable as a dog, its slavering jaws open wide, its eyes wildly large, reflecting fires of hell.

Another shiver of recognition went through Thomas. This was the beast that tent preacher so long ago had described, the messenger from hell who waited for the wicked on the other side of death and, clamping them in its fiery jaws, ran with them to deposit them down into the roasting fires below.

That wail was what this creature, the Hound, would sound like, had sounded like in Thomas's mind so long ago.

Again, Mullin shivered. Out loud, he berated himself for his foolishness, was glad that none of his men, even Reeves, was here to see him. He had prided himself on his toughness, and here he was, cowering in the dark because of a story told when he was a child.

Still, he heard that wail in his mind, saw the Hound, could not separate the two. The unearthly sound, the Indians had names for it, the circle of bones, the stalking demon. What if—

*No.*

Physically, he willed himself to stop thinking such foolish thoughts. They were tales to scare children, superstition. He had long since outgrown them, and knew that he was stalking a man, and nothing more.

Still . . .

For the first time since he could remember, Thomas Mullin felt alone. All through his years in the Army, he had formed a veneer around himself, added layers of toughness to it, because of his color, because of his pride, and had always told himself, as Ames, his friend in the War, from New York, had told him, "Hold what you have, very tight, and it will not get away." What he had held was himself, and he had held so tight to his pride, to his sense of worth, of accomplishment, that he had forgotten what it was like to be lonely, to be just one creature outside of the Army, alone under the stars, with all of creation against you. Being Negro, he had thought there was only one kind of separation, but this was another, and greater one, that every man felt: the separation from all things.

Despite his iron will, Thomas shivered again.

A wail sounded, very far away, and he started.

*Coyote.*

He laughed.

His iron will returned. He read the story of *The Hound of the Baskervilles,* all four parts, alone, in the night, under the stars.

It wasn't until morning, when the sun was kissing the day, that hell opened up once more, and he heard the chilling sound again.

# *Chapter Eleven*

Two Suns Rising slept uneasily. The spirit world was alive this night, the ghosts released during the terrible storm of hot ice still walking the earth. Two Suns Rising could feel them all around him. Last night had been a Letting Go, a release, and most of the spirits, he feared, had been evil, coming down in the form of clouds and not yet dissipated.

The clearing sky, the stars, would draw them back up eventually, but they must be very strong demons to still walk the earth with coming day. Two Suns had heard their leader, their Shaman, wailing in the night above him, cries mingled with the thunder clouds, and he listened for more cries. But, so far, there were none, which made Two Suns even more uneasy, because, when the cries came, they might be even more fierce than they had been. Evil Shamans did not like to leave the Earth once freed, and their wrath while walking among the living could be terrible indeed.

Two Suns could not help thinking that his Chief had brought this trouble on. Though this was something Two Suns would never say, he knew that other braves felt that this excursion into the land of the Buffalo Soldiers was foolhardy and doomed to fail, and that, rather than revenge and glory, all of them would receive only death, and a further blow to pride. Victorio's memory was already a fading one, except to the old men, but it was they who had decreed that once again the Mescalero Apaches would be free of their Agency and rise to greatness. Two Suns had been only eleven when Victorio fell five years before, but his only memories were of flight and fear. He remembered the Buffalo Soldiers as fierce enemies, and had no wish to see their dark faces again.

But here he was, looking for Waiting Moon, his cousin, while the forty warriors waited in the Eagle Mountains to the west. Waiting Moon had been sent because of his fleetness, but when he had failed to return immediately Two Suns had set out after him. He, too, rode a Lipan mount and wore Lipan dress, and, if caught, would play the foolhardy youth out for a lark, hunting against his elders' wishes—

He heard the cry of the demon, close by.

The blood went cold in Two Suns' veins. It sounded as if the demon was just above him, on the top of this mountain. His horse began to snort, and he rose quickly, quieting it, as the cry of the demon came again.

Dawn was finding the sky. Silent as a doe, Two Suns crept from his rock cutout to the ledge twenty feet away. He turned his eyes and looked up.

A gasp caught in his throat.

There, not fifty feet above him, outlined starkly against the lightening sky, at the summit of the mountain, was the demon. As Two Suns watched, the demon wailed again, hands uplifted, thin as a wraith, nearly naked. It beat at its head, then held its arms high overhead and turned to face the rising sun.

The demon threw back its head, and again it wailed, a terrible sound that made Two Suns cover his ears.

Paralyzed with fright, Two Suns watched the Shaman cackle at the coming sun, then suddenly fall to the ground. It beat its fists, crying out, making unintelligible words. There was a moment of silence, and then Two Suns saw the demon appear suddenly at the edge of the summit, head cocked out, seeming to peer at him.

The demon wailed down at him.

Galvanized, Two Suns ran for his horse, pulled himself onto it, kicked it away from the side of the mountain.

Behind him, he heard a scramble of rocks.

He looked back to see the demon jump from its summit, land on a rock ledge, jump down again, stand in the place Two Suns had just vacated.

"Wait!" the demon screamed at him, in the white man's tongue.

Two Suns reared his horse up, turned around.

The demon stood in the shadow of a rock, regarding him oddly, turning its head from side to side.

"Don't go," it said. It laughed, taking a step forward, still moving its head in that reptilian fashion.

Two Suns stepped his horse back, to keep distance between himself and the demon.

The demon stepped out of shadow, into rising sunlight.

It turned its head deliberately up, staring straight into the sun, and smiled. Its face was burned nearly black.

"I own it, now," it said, and laughed. Again, it took a step forward.

Two Suns kept his feet snugged into the sides of his mount, ready to flee.

The demon turned toward him again, head cocked, eyes nearly to the side.

"You're older than seventeen, aren't you? I can tell."

The demon sprang at him.

Two Suns reined his horse around and kicked into it.

The demon, scrabbling like a monkey, nearly got a hand on him. Two Suns looked back to see the demon gone.

He moved the horse down the path, as fast as he could.

There was a spill of rocks above, and Two Suns glanced up to see the demon on the rock shelf above him, catching up. The Shaman made little laughing sounds.

"Oh, yes, more than seventeen."

Two Suns saw a rockier path, steeper, but away from the rock ledge. He angled his mount toward it. Below was a flat area that led down to the canyon.

The horse slid its hooves, tried to slow up. Two Suns guided it to a clearer spot and they moved steadily down the slope.

Behind him, Two Suns heard a whoop. He looked back to see the demon running wildly down the slope toward him, leaping wildly.

"Yes!" the Shaman said.

Two Suns' horse hit a patch of loose stones and slipped forward, throwing the Mescalero brave to the ground.

On his back, Two Suns looked up to see the flank of the horse, the demon rearing up on the horse's back, then driving a long blade deep under the horse's throat as he pulled back sharply on the reins.

A river of blood poured down over Two Suns. Then, the demon was standing astride him, looking down, angling his wide, blank eyes from side to side.

"Yes," the demon tittered.

Two Suns saw the blade flash in the sun as it dropped toward him.

# Chapter Twelve

Murphy looked no better when they were ready to leave the next morning at nine than he had the day before. Most of the packing and provisioning had been left to Reeves, and he heard from Rivers that there had been another all-night poker game in the officer's quarters and that the Pinkerton men had done no better than they had before.

"They're bad drinkers," Rivers said, "and bad drunks. I'd watch out for the one named Porter, if I was you. He doesn't drink much himself, but from what I heard he fed that Captain of theirs all night, and runs the show. Once Murphy gets drunk Porter does whatever he wants. I'm told he made a lot of . . . disparaging comments about the soldiers here, if you follow me."

Reeves regarded Rivers solemnly. "I think I do."

"Just so's you know, boy. Keep your two eyes open."

"I will."

Rivers winked, patting a saddlebag on Reeves's mount. "And since you got all those white boys going with you, I thought it was all right to pack a little extra coffee. Lieutenant Mullin wouldn't take enough with him when he set out, so you can split it with him when you see him."

"Thanks, Rivers."

Rivers walked away, waving his hand. "Don't thank me. Just be careful."

"Yes," Reeves said, and, after Rivers had disappeared into the shadows of the stable, the private rechecked the rifle in its sling on his mount, and the sidearm he had decided to wear for this trip.

After eyeing their horses with trepidation, the Pinkerton men headed to Captain Seavers's office for a final talk.

"Make sure that stuff's tied down real good, boy," Porter said to Reeves as he left. He smiled crookedly. "Wouldn't want to have to tell your commanding officer anything bad about you wooly-heads."

Reeves stood staring after Porter as Lieutenant Adams approached.

"Got what you need, Reeves," Adams said. He handed Reeves a packet of papers, which Reeves put into his jacket pocket. "There's some interesting things in there. Seems there have been a whole lot of disappearances over the last year and a half, most of them unexplained. The whole year before that, there were only two, and one of them turned out to be a mountain lion attack, the other a little girl who wandered away from a settlement and fell into a ravine."

"Thank you, Sir. I know Lieutenant Mullin will be grateful."

Adams said, "Hell, Reeves, I wish I could go with you. I asked Seavers, but he wouldn't let me. I think he's going to do something about those Mescaleros of Thomas's, soon as you leave. I think I've got him ready to get me to handle that. Better than sitting here watching all these damn incompetents not do their jobs."

"Thank you again, Sir," Reeves said.

"Trooper," Adams said, "mind if I ask you a question?"

"No, I don't mind, Sir."

"I don't know if you're aware that I fought for the Confederacy during the War. My family had slaves. Growing up, I never thought about it. I was young, and I would have gladly died so that my daddy and his friends could keep their slaves." Adams hesitated, rubbed his chin. "What I want to know is, how come you and the other Negro boys are so damn good at your job? Just about every white man out here is second rate. We've been through twenty commanders in the last ten years, and, except for Grierson, I could take or leave most of 'em. I watched Thomas go through hell trying to get promoted, even after the stuff he did during the war with Victorio. Did he tell you he saved the lives of three white officers? Even after all that, it took help out East to get him promoted past Sergeant."

"Your question was, why are we so good at our job?"

"I don't know if it was really a question, Reeves. It's just that, when I grew up there were slaves, and that was the world, that was the way things were. Now we have a different world. Why the hell doesn't everybody, inside the Army and out, live in the world we got, instead of trying to make believe we still got the old one?"

"I can't answer that, Sir."

"Neither can I, Reeves. But every once in a while, I have to ask the question."

"I can answer your original question though, Sir, about why we're so good at our job."

Adams rubbed his chin again. "Go ahead."

"It's because that's what our world is now, Sir."

Adams put his hand briefly on Reeves shoulder, shook his head. "That's why I get along so well with you fellas, maybe. Say hello to Thomas for me, Reeves."

"I will, Sir."

Adams walked away, still shaking his head.

By the time the Pinkerton men were ready to go it was almost eleven o'clock, which meant there would be little hope of finding Thomas until late the next day. Reeves frowned to see that Murphy looked better, which meant that he must have already had his first drink of the day. Reeves' suspicion was confirmed when Porter slipped his flask back into his hip pocket as he approached.

"What's the matter, boy, never seen a detective before?" Porter said, grinning.

"Let's get out of here," Murphy said, with authority. "We've already wasted enough time. We've got a job to do."

"That we do," Porter said, still grinning. "That we do."

Porter and Murphy were adequate riders, but it was obvious that Sommers and Chaney had never been on a horse. After an hour, they still had the Fort well in sight behind them, and Sommers and Chaney were already complaining. Murphy told them to be quiet.

Secretly, Reeves relished the saddle sores the tenderfoots would sport the next morning, after a day of riding and an uncomfortable sleep.

They followed Limpia Creek, which was, after the recent scarcity of rain, completely dry in some spots. A few cattle grazed near scant watering holes, and in one location the water was deep enough to cover the hooves of a small herd of barrel-chested deer.

"Venison!" Porter said excitedly, stopping to unsling his rifle. But the deer, who had watched impassively, suddenly bolted and were gone, bolting zig-zag into the dry grass on the far side of the creek.

"That's enough," Murphy said, glaring at Porter until the rifle had been re-slung. "We don't have time for foolishness."

"Seems we had plenty of time last night, *Sir.*" Porter said. "If I remember correctly, there was a three-quarters full bottle that was empty by daylight, and a little more of your monthly salary in that bluebelly Forsen's pocket."

Sommers and Chaney, moving uneasily in their saddles, managed to grin.

Murphy, glaring toward anger, suddenly softened and managed to smile. "I still say that Corporal was cheating," he said, holding his hand out toward Porter, who had already produced his hip flask.

"That he was, Captain," Porter said. "But you were having such a good time, I thought it best to let it slide."

The four Pinkerton men laughed, Murphy breaking off to tilt the flask to his mouth. He lowered it, sloshing its contents uncertainly.

"Don't worry, Captain, I brought some of my own provisions along." Porter smiled. "I had a little talk with that cheating Corporal after you went to bed, and he compensated us for your losses." Porter dug into the saddlebag behind him, drew out a long, full whiskey bottle.

Sommers hooted. "Go get 'em, Captain!"

Murphy smiled, took another short shot from the flask and handed it back to Porter. "Good work," he said. "Now let's get some real work done."

They rode another hour, until Chaney said he had to stop. Murphy readily agreed. Reeves thought to protest, thinking about how slowly they were going, but kept his lips sealed.

They dismounted near a clutch of stunted cottonwoods. After tying the horses, Porter headed immediately for the bare shade of the largest tree.

"I'd check that area for copperheads," Reeves said.

Porter turned on him, anger flaring.

"You do it . . . boy."

Reeves moved past Porter, ducked under the low branches, kicked at a flat rock near the bole of the tree. Something long hissed and slithered out. Quickly, Reeves brought the heel of his boot down on the snake's head, crushing it.

Porter had lost some of his color. Sommers laughed, "Would have bit your ass good, Jimmy!"

Porter quickly regained his composure, ducked into the shade and sat down against the tree.

"Did I say the area was free of copperheads?" Reeves said flatly.

Porter started to rise, until he saw the slight smile on Reeves's face. "I believe you did, *boy*," he said.

Reeves, still smiling, shrugged and walked away.

Murphy, Reeves saw, was already at the new bottle of whiskey. That was a very bad sign. Here it was barely noon, and already the Pinkerton Captain was long past sober. Reeves also noticed that the others were doing nothing about it. Sommers and Chaney were eating beans, and had a deck of cards opened between them, playing blackjack. Porter, who had abandoned his resting spot, was staring back at the direction they'd come sullenly.

Taking a deep breath, Reeves approached Porter. "Listen," he said, as diplomatically as he could, "I should tell you that the heat out here is going to make your Captain feel his liquor faster. If he keeps it up, we'll have to stop by early afternoon and find a rock wall out of the sun to let him sober up."

Porter looked at Reeves stonily. Reeves had the feeling that the other man was trying to pretend he wasn't there.

"Listen . . ." Reeves tried again.

"You hear that, Captain?" Porter called to Murphy. "The black-and-bluebelly here says you're drunk, and he doesn't like it."

"That's not what I said . . ." Reeves began.

Murphy was staring at him. He capped the bottle he held and slipped it back into Porter's saddlebag. "Perhaps he's right," he said, surprisingly mild.

"But Captain . . ." Porter said.

"Let's mount up and go," Murphy said evenly.

Chaney and Sommers were already heading for their horses. Reeves noted that they had left their empty bean cans.

"We really should clean camp," Reeves said.

"I said mount up," Murphy said, and Reeves saw that though the Captain's voice was quiet, it was not without malice.

The four Pinkerton men were already heading north when Reeves had mounted and moved after, catching up to discreetly lead them.

As Private Reeves feared, they didn't make it through the afternoon. Murphy was thoughtfully quiet for a while, but after another two hours of riding Porter refilled his hip flask from the bottle in his saddlebag and passed it to the Captain. Without comment, Murphy began to drink from it. Reeves noted that Murphy was the kind of man who had come to accept alcohol as second nature.

"Porter," Reeves said, but Porter answered without turning toward him.

"Shut up, darkie."

Chaney sniggered, and Murphy said nothing with his voice, but plenty by tipping the flask back up to his mouth and drinking deep.

They were in hill shadow for a while, but when the wide sweep of the Limpia Canyon opened in front of them the direct sun beat down mercilessly. Reeves estimated it was nearly three o'clock.

Reeves watched the Captain closely. There was no shade to steer them towards. It didn't take long for the sun to do its work. Murphy began to sweat profusely, wiping at his brow with a handkerchief, then drinking slightly from his flask. Suddenly he slumped in his saddle, began to tilt to one side.

Reeves and Porter were next to him quickly. The Captain collapsed into Reeves. They halted. Porter dismounted and ran around to help the Captain down. Porter gave a quick, anxious glance at Reeves and lay Murphy flat on the ground, shading him with his horse, opening his collar.

"Give him a little water," Reeves said. "Just a little."

"We'll have to stop," Chaney said laconically, and Sommers shrugged and dismounted, heading for the creek. In a few minutes they saw him washing his face in the barely running water, then returning to pull out his pack of cards.

"Believe you owe me money, Sommers," he said, and the two Pinkerton men found a shelf of rock and began to play cards.

"I don't like where we are," Reeves said.

Porter cut him a sharp look. "Where the hell you want to go?"

"If we head northwest, there's some high ground where we can at least make camp. There's no real shade for another twenty miles."

"We can't go twenty miles with Murphy like this."

"That's why we'll hit the high ground and stay there."

"We'll stay right here," Porter said.

"That's not a good idea." Reeves tried to keep his voice even and reasonable. "It'd be better to get on high ground before nightfall. It'll cool off quicker, and give us a better look around."

"At what? Who the hell cares where we are?"

Reeves spoke slowly. "We've got renegade Mescaleros and a killer in the area. I think it would be a good idea."

Porter's eyes were murderous. "All right, darkie." He began to haul Murphy up, accepting Reeves's help to drape him over his saddle. "But remember who's in charge."

Porter turned to Chaney and Sommers. "Fill your canteens," he snapped. "We're heading into the hills."

Without another word, Porter mounted his horse, holding the reins from Murphy's mount, and set off at a slow pace until Reeves had caught up and quietly pulled ahead to lead them.

By sundown they were well encamped. Murphy had recovered a bit, and Reeves was horrified to see the Captain ask for, and receive from Porter, a fresh drink from the flask.

They ate a meal. Afterwards, as Sommers and Chaney argued over cards, Reeves scouted their position. They were on a low shelf a couple of hundred feet off the canyon plain, with a good view of all four horizons. From here Lincoln could see to where Lieutenant Mullin should be in the northwest. He truly missed the older man's company, and made a silent wish on Sirius, the dog star just rising through the hazy twilight, that he would join up with him soon. He made a vow that he would ask Thomas to teach him to read.

Instead of getting quieter as the sun set, the Pinkerton men got louder. Sommers and Chaney, it seemed, had their own source of whiskey, a half-full bottle which they kept winning from one another, toasting each card game with mutual drinks. Porter had begun to drink, also, slowly, as if stoking his fires. Murphy, who had recovered his wits to the point where they could be drowned in alcohol again, was truly drunk, sharing Porter's bottle and telling loud stories about his early life in St. Louis. All of which led, finally, to a scene Reeves imagined had been played out many times among these four men: their Captain breaking into sobs at the mention of the loss of his wife and daughter to fever, many years before, the subsequent loss of his good desk job in the Pinkerton office and a gradual slide to his present position. Sommers and Chaney seemed not even to be listening, and Porter only looked up when the story found its inevitable end in the Captain giving a final oath and then falling asleep into his own arms. Porter helped lay him out flat, then threw a blanket over Murphy and immediately abandoned him.

Reeves felt Porter approaching, then turned to confront him. Porter had brought a length of rope with him.

"Any more suggestions, darkie?"

Reeves was close enough to smell whiskey on Porter's breath. "I'm just doing my job."

Porter laughed. "Your job? Your job is to pick cotton, shuffle, and grin. Is your first name really Lincoln?"

"That's right."

Porter guffawed. "I like that. Where I come from, you know whose birthday we celebrate? John Wilkes Booth. You really think that bastard Lincoln freed you?" He spat. "You know Lincoln was really a darkie? Did you ever hear that? They found black under the white paint on his face. He was black—and ugly."

Reeves tensed, seeing the other man's eyes darken.

"I should hang you right here." Porter's voice became menacingly loud. Chaney and Sommers stopped their card game and watched impassively.

"Should I hang him, boys?"

Chaney snorted a laugh. "Sure, Porter. Anything you want."

Sommers dealt another hand, and Chaney watched Reeves and Porter for a moment before rejoining the game. "He's just a darkie, right, Porter? Even the Army can spare a darkie." Chaney laughed.

"We'll back you up, Porter," Sommers said. "We'll tell 'em the Mescaleros got him. Never mind my abolitionist past. Only one problem, though."

"What's that?" Porter said.

"Ain't no tree."

Chaney guffawed. "That's right, Porter. Only tree we seen today had a copperhead under it."

"Shut up," Porter snapped. "There's other ways."

"Like what?" Sommers said.

Porter said, "We tie his hands, put the rope around his neck and let a horse pull him. Saw it once in Wyoming."

"Was that a darkie too?" Chaney said. "Or a copperhead?"

Sommers and Chaney both laughed, dealing another hand of twenty-one.

"Put your hands behind your back," Porter said to Reeves.

Reeves went for his sidearm. But Porter had already swung for him, and knocked him to the ground. Reeves nearly had his gun out of its holster but Porter was strong and yanked it out of Reeves's grip, tossing it away into darkness. Reeves was hit twice in the face, then was turned over. He felt himself being tied.

Thinking quickly, he stiffened his wrists, angling them out from one another, making the bond loose when he released tension.

Chaney laughed, but Sommers said, "Hey, enough's enough, Jimmy."

"I said shut up," Porter said. He cut the rope at the knot on Reeves's wrists, fashioned the end into a noose and slipped it over Reeves's neck, notched it tight before hauling Reeves to his feet.

"Hey, this is no joke, Jimmy," Sommers said. "It's all right to fool with they boy, I'm sure he won't say anything if you let him go now."

"I told you to keep your mouth shut."

Sommers had risen from the card game; he walked to Porter and put a hand on his arm. "You're drunk," he said, "and you don't know what you're doing."

Porter knocked him down with his forearm. "I said—"

Captain Murphy made a loud, choking sound from the edge of the camp where he lay. Sommers got up, joined Chaney at the Captain's side.

"Jesus, he ain't breathing right!" Chaney said.

Sommers lay Murphy down flat, but the Captain was thrashing so badly they couldn't keep him still. Sommers tried to get Murphy's mouth open, without success. Suddenly, Murphy gave a hitching gasp and his eyes rolled up into his head.

"He's dying!" Chaney shouted.

Porter hauled Reeves by the rope over to where Murphy lay.

Sommers looked up from Murphy and said to Porter, "He's dead, Jimmy."

"He drank too much," Reeves said solemnly. He looked hard at Porter. "You let him drink again after getting sunstroke today. He drank himself to death."

"He's been trying to do it for a long time," Porter said. "Well . . ."

"Jesus, they'll blame us for sure!" Chaney said in panic, rising.

Porter looked at Sommers. "Now you got a choice, Sam. Either we hang the darkie and blame the Captain's death on him, or swing ourselves."

Sommers, agitated, looked from Porter to Reeves. "Jimmy—"

"Ain't no third choice, Sam."

"I'm with you," Chaney said quickly, standing to join Porter. "No other way we don't get the blame."

"Lord Almighty," Sommers said. "I just can't—"

"Just take a little walk, do a little lookout," Porter said slowly. "We'll take care of it."

"My Lord," Sommers said.

He rose slowly and walked away, giving Reeves a final, haunted look.

Porter grinned at Reeves. "So much for President Lincoln's abolitionist. Kind of makes it sweeter, this way."

Reeves began to protest. Porter knocked him to the ground as Chaney quickly tied the other end of the rope leading to his neck to the saddle horn of Reeves's horse. Chaney then held Reeves down while Porter stripped the horse of saddlebags and rifle.

"All right, let him go," Porter snapped.

Chaney released Reeves. Porter slapped Lincoln's mount, shouting for it to run. It took off at a gallop.

Porter hooted with glee as Reeves was dragged past him.

"Good-bye, darkie!"

Choking, Reeves saw Porter's grinning face as he was pulled

past, felt the kick of Porter's boot in his side as he was pulled off into the night.

The horse had dragged Reeves fifty feet before he was able to twist his bonds loose enough to work a hand free. Porter had been drunk enough to let Reeves give himself plenty of slack.

Still, it was close. The rope around his neck was plenty tight. He was beginning to lose consciousness when he finally reached up to grab at the rope and pull the pressure off his throat. He gasped, pulled in a long gulp of air, twisted the rope away from his neck.

A sharp rock dug under him, into his arm and then ribs.

He almost released the rope. With an iron will he held on, reached his other hand up and pulled the rope up over his head and flipped it free.

With a gasp he let go.

He heard the horse gallop on as he tumbled to a stop.

He lay breathing hard for a full minute. Slowly, he turned over onto his back and looked up into the sky.

Far away, he heard the vague sounds of the horse running into the night on one side, Porter and Sommers shouting on the other.

Finally, he pulled himself to his feet, stumbled in the direction of the horse, away from the sound of human voices.

He walked as long and far as he could. The stars wheeled slowly overhead. There was a long, burning pain in his right side; whenever he straightened, dull fire told him that at least one rib was cracked. His legs and arms were bruised. There was a cut over one eye that eventually stopped bleeding. His lip was also cut, and for awhile he tasted blood.

Finally, he could go no farther. All sounds had faded behind him. The horse had not found him, and he gave up hope, at least until the morning, of coming to where it had stopped. His low calls to it had gone unanswered.

He dropped to his knees, breath running out of him in a gasp.

The burning pain in his side had worsened. His hand had come up wet with blood from his shirt. He feared his side had been pierced.

He lay down on his back, breathing weakly, looking up at the sky.

The stars were blocked.

At first he thought it was a cloud. But then his eyes focused on the outline of a human form, with stars mantling it.

"Lieutenant Mullin?" he said, hopefully.

The figure was silent, a black form blocking the black sky.

"Oh God," Lincoln said. "Porter."

Still, the form was silent.

"Who . . ." Lincoln said, the strength running out of him, unconsciousness coming to claim him.

The figure remained mute.

Then, as Private Reeves's own blackness was dropping down on him, turning the burning in his side to a vague, faraway dream pain, making the world go away, he heard a voice, which must have been from another world, because it was so eerily gentle, so meaningless, speak gently to him, "Are you older than seventeen?"

# *Chapter Thirteen*

There was no more screaming. He knew the blessing of blindness for what it was.

For now, even the Sun had come to worship him, to show fear at his presence.

Oh, there had been fear in the beginning. Thoughts of The Woman had assaulted him. He imagined she had risen from her bed, faceless, and come at him with red-hot pokers, one in each hand, just out of the fireplace, driving them deep into his eyes—seeking, perhaps, to burn herself into his brain. Those were his first thoughts. To see the world suddenly black, it was natural that he had first thought of curse instead of homage. Blind. How would he do his work, fight the day and kick the bones of those who had turned to dried mud, if he could not see? His battle with the Sun had been lost, and despair had filled him. He had dropped to the ground, and the Sun had burned into his skin, making it like the surface of the Sun itself, seeking to turn him to dried mud, seeking to strike him down to mortality. He had cried, thinking the battle over, that the Sun had defeated him.

Weeping, he had slept.

Blind and burned, he had awakened in the night, feeling the coolness of the desert around him, sensing the absence of the hated enemy the Sun—and then true despair had filled him. He could not even see the night! True blackness, blackness in his head robbing him of the blackness of his night—this he could not stand.

He had cried, crawling on his belly like a dog to the edge of the mountain, and made the decision to give in to the Sun and throw himself to the rocks below.

But then he made a glorious discovery. Standing there, at the edge of the world, poised for destruction, he found that—glory of glories—at the corner of his eyes, he could see. There, at the edge of his eyes, he saw—stars!

Stars haloed his eyes, grew more distinct, then ringed his eyes gloriously until they faded with coming day.

And then—most wonderful discovery of all—the Sun had come—and he had defeated it!

For there he stood on the edge of the world, facing the East, and when the Sun rose it did not burn into his eyes, but hid itself from his sight! Even more glorious—when he looked straight at it, the Sun became, in each of his eyes, a black sun!

*The Sun belonged to him!*

He had screamed in triumph, and then, looking down, away from the dark of the Sun, angling his eyes to the side away from the black circles where he could see, he spied an Indian brave waiting for death below!

Glory of glories! What a wonderful offering! How he had relished the fear and awe in the Indian's eyes, watching the young brave around the permanent black suns in the center of his eyes, a reflection of himself, because he had become the Black Sun itself!

Oh, how the young Indian had died, so slowly, to his homage, the rending of flesh, parts to return to dried mud, to dust . . .

And now he would find the ones who had desecrated the first Indian's grave, had dared interrupt his work. For he was God . . .

This new night was long, and he went about his work. His memory was a good one. There was an old man buried at the toe of a canyon offshoot; he found the marker and it was dried mud. He kicked it to dust. There were two men nearby, he remembered the high, clear night, their campfire, their laughter, sleeping under the stars, and he found their markers. "You were mud, wet dust, and now you are dust," he said, crushing their powdery skulls beneath his boot, watching the plumes of dried innards rise and fall to the earth. There was another nearby—

Off on the other side of the canyon, came the faintest of sounds.

He imagined he would have heard it earlier, had his work not taken his mind. There it came again. The cry of a man, the whinny of a horse. He listened, head cocked, and it repeated, perceptively closer. He stood still as a bird, continuing to listen, and then the horse drew closer and it was time for him to look.

He climbed a steep slope, hands and feet scrabbling, and perched on the edge. His eyes around the black suns were sensitive to the night. At first he saw nothing; but then, off across the canyon plain below, a couple of miles off, he saw a horse.

He scrambled quickly down, chose a spot to intercept the horse and made for it. There was a column of rocks the steed would pass through, and he positioned himself between it.

The land sloped down away from him; he lost sight of the mount but he could hear its ragged breath, its desperate hoofbeats.

The horse rose in front of him, dashed through the rock portals—

"Whoa!" he said.

The horse was past him, mouth foaming, a look of fear in its wide eyes. He reached for it, missed the saddle, felt his hands move down a long rope and hold on. The horse pulled him to the ground, but he continued to hold tight.

Suddenly the horse reared up and stopped, huffing breath, frightened.

"Whoa there, boy," he soothed, reeling the rope slowly toward him. It was bound to the saddle. He examined the end he held. It was a closed noose.

He took the horse by its reins, untied the rope, looped it around his waist and retied it, drew the horse's face close to his.

"You all right?" he said, gently.

The horse huffed breath, stamped a foot, responded to his stroking.

"Good boy."

He drew his long blade out, held the horse gently under the chin and brought the knife deeply into the back of its throat.

The horse's eyes went wide and it dropped in a shower of blood to its knees.

In a moment it was dead.

He knelt down beside it, made his mark, and patted its flank.

"All creatures of the earth are mine," he said, and then dipped his hand deep into the cavity of the cut throat and drank, feeling the warmth fill his throat as he swallowed.

The rider was easy to find. He followed the horse's trail back until a cut in the canyon showed where it had veered off from the plain. There was a shelf of hills at the horizon. He headed toward it. After two hour's walk he detected movement at the corner of his eye and stopped to let the figure in the distance become clear to him.

The figure moved slowly, staggered forward and then stopped, staggered forward again. It was a half mile off. He sat on his haunches, rolled a cigarette, smoked it.

Finally, the figure dropped to the ground, a quarter mile in front of him.

He discarded the cigarette, approached slowly.

The figure rolled onto its back, strained for breath. It wore the uniform of the Army of the Sun, of the fort in the distance.

He stood over the figure, looked down.

The figure stared up at him, muttered a name, another name.

He said, "Are you more than seventeen?" His hand reached smoothly for his blade.

His eyes registered something that made him stop.

He moved his eyes from side to side, bent down to look closer, could not believe what he saw.

"Who are you?" he said, half in awe.

The figure was breathing shallowly.

He knelt next to the figure, examined his face. There were cuts on the lip and over one eye. He felt the skin, gently. Still, he thought he was not seeing correctly.

Black. The figure's skin was black.

He put his hand to the skin, pinched it, drew his fingers away and held them up close to examine.

The black had not come off.

*Black.*

A soldier of the night.

This was not a soldier of the Army of the Sun—this was *his* soldier!

Oh, joy complete!

He shook the soldier gently awake; the soldier groaned and then opened his eyes and looked groggily up at him.

"Where do you come from?" he said gently.

"Fort . . ." the soldier said, and then his eyes closed and again he slept.

*The fort!*

Again, he shook the soldier awake. "Why is your color black?"

For a moment the soldier looked clearly at him, then began to slip back to unconsciousness.

"Why is your color black!"

"All black. . . ." the soldier said.

All of them! A fort of soldiers of the night!

Here to fight his war, to bring night to all the world!

He whooped for joy, and kissed the soldier on the forehead. "Don't worry," he said, and then, binding the soldier hand and foot, he drew him up over his shoulders, carrying him strongly, and went off to find a place for the day.

# *Chapter Fourteen*

Thomas's first day in Wild Rose Pass was wasted on false leads. Twice, he thought he had found grave sites similar to the Indian's, but both sites revealed, on closer inspection, nothing but a chance arrangement of sun-bleached stones. He began to believe he might be chasing a spirit after all. That night, he was too frustrated even to read.

The next day, deeper into Limpia Canyon, brought much better luck. He found the first of three graves before noon. At first he thought it was the Senator's son, because the grave was fairly fresh. But it was not fresh, only freshly-uncovered, the circle with arrow pointing west, shallow and perfect. The bones in the grave were old, broken to dust. Thomas estimated that they belonged to an old man. The innards had long since decomposed.

There were two more nearby. Neither of those were the boy, either. These had also been newly uncovered. Thomas was sure that if Reeves obtained that list he had asked for, there would be listed on it two young cowboys. The killer had crushed the skulls.

Thomas wondered just how many other graves like this were hidden in the hills, low mountains and canyons around him. From the looks of these two, whoever it was doing this had been at it for at least a couple of years.

Thomas thought of his eerie feelings of the night before, but before a chill could rise up his back he had banished it.

This was a man he was after, not a spirit.

There were telltale signs, now. None of the four graves had held a child. None held a woman. All were buried in the same manner, in a shallow circular grave, bones marking the perimeter, skull at the top, facing west.

Thomas racked his brains, tried to think of some Indian tribe that buried the dead this way, but found nothing in his memory.

What was it Holmes was always telling Watson?

*After you have eliminated the impossible, whatever remains, however improbable, must be the truth.*

On the third grave, the shallow circle in which the second cowboy was buried, Thomas found a clue.

He tried to follow some of Holmes's methods, searching the gravesite on his hands and knees. He found, sheltered under a yellow rose cactus, the heel of a bootprint, dried to hardness. On further examination he found another, a partial print for the opposite heel of the same sort of boot, which had been exposed to the elements. He imagined his one good print had been made just after rain, possibly the preceding spring, because the ground had been soft enough to take a well-defined print, but not wet enough to destroy it.

He went to his saddlebag, drew out a leather satchel filled with plaster and a square tin box. He returned with his canteen to the bootprint, opened the tin box, which was empty, filled it halfway with plaster, and added water from the canteen. He mixed it with a stick, then poured the wet plaster into the bootprint, pressing it gently out to the edges.

While he waited, he drew out a survey map of the Davis Mountains and marked the areas where he had, so far, found bodies. There was a great empty distance between the Indian's grave he had found on Sleeping Lion Mountain and those in Limpia Canyon. But he was immediately struck by the partial arc the three graves he had found today made.

Sketching lightly, using the arc as a guide, he drew a partial circle, the point passing almost precisely through the gravesite on Sleeping Lion Mountain.

He completed the circle, and sat staring at it. It occurred to him that perhaps they were dealing with an Apache, or Apaches, after all. The Apaches always conducted their campaigns following a precise pattern, sometimes an *X*, sometimes a square. The circle was a common one. He was also struck by the fact that the circle had Fort Davis in its middle, but skirted it widely. Could a single Apache, or small band, have been acting in the Davis Mountains for the past couple of years, quietly killing stray settlers and cowboys? After all, the Mescaleros were nearby now; could these murders have been some sort of prelude to new Mescalero action against Fort Davis?

He didn't like it. There was something inconsistent and eerie about it. The bootprint he had found had not come from a boot worn by an Apache.

As Holmes said, *After you have eliminated the impossible . . .*

He had been staring at one section of the map, and now he saw what he was looking at. On the western edge of the circle, just outside its perimeter, sat Flat Top, the highest, and flattest, peak in the Davis Mountains. It was a beautiful summit, the air crystal clear at the top, a perfect place—

Thomas sketched in a line leading straight west from the circle through Flat Top.

*After you have eliminated the impossible . . .*

The drawing he had made now looked exactly like the graves he had uncovered, a circle (of bones) with an addition (the skull, filled with the innards) facing west.

He now knew that all the bodies would be buried along the line of this circle.

The question was: where would he find the Senator's son?

He studied the map, looking for a pattern. He had the new grave he had found, on Sleeping Lion Mountain; he had two older graves. Could there be a pattern to the way the dead were buried?

There was just too much blank space on his circle. And, he wondered, what could be buried on Flat Top?

After a while his eyes began to ache. He folded the map, put it away, and went to retrieve his plaster cast of the bootprint.

He carefully lifted the cast out of the ground, brushed it off.

It was perfect; it even showed a chip out of one edge of the boot's heel, and the wear of the heel from right to left.

He packed everything carefully away. Suddenly, very badly, he wanted to see the information that Trooper Reeves had gathered for him. He wanted to study that list of disappearances. He had no doubt there was a vital clue in it somewhere.

He mounted his horse, made his decision. At best, the Pinkerton men and Reeves were heading toward him now. He could meet them halfway.

He had to see that list as soon as possible.

*After you have eliminated the impossible . . .*

# *Chapter Fifteen*

The Eagle Mountains were well behind them.

It was time to ride. There was no more time to wait for brash young ones, with no feeling for the past or for the pride of their ancestors, to return with news. Pretorio had heard enough of their womanly discussion over the past weeks. For five years, he had planned his revenge on the white eyes, and especially on the Buffalo Soldiers, and nothing—not treaty, not the whining of youths not fit to be called braves, not the women still wailing for the deaths of their fathers five years before—would stop him. They were Mescalero, and even if the white eyes said that a place called New Mexico was their home, and that they could not leave it again, they would do so, treaties be cursed, and they would fight as Pretorio's great brother Victorio had.

And this time they would win.

This time, there would be no defeat. It was foretold: that one would come after Victorio, a great warrior who would do what the great Victorio could not, unite the tribes and rise again, driving white man and Buffalo Soldier out of the hunting grounds, and sacred mountains, and once again things would be as they had been before.

"In two days we will know," Pretorio said.

"We already know," Springs of Life, his medicine man said. They looked, together from their horses, out over the plain where their band of two hundred had begun to move east. It was Springs of Life who had read the signs, in the air, in the water, in the land, and said that the time was now. "The white man thinks this is a time of peace, so we make war. It was written, and the signs are with us. In the peaceful, warm desert, ice rain falls. We saw it from the mountain. It falls on the white man, and the Buffalo Soldier, and we will fall like ice rain on them, and drive them into the ground where their blood will make water for the seeds that grow grass. There will be no more Buffalo Soldier—only buffalo. This, too, is foretold."

Pretorio turned to his companion and said, "But you and I are old. We remember the foretellings. These young ones, they remember only fear, and running from the Buffalo Soldiers, and defeat. They do not know how to be warriors. They wail like women, and talk about the reservation as if it were home. How do we make them fight?"

"You know the answer already," Springs of Life said.

Pretorio nodded. "I know they have it within them. But I fear it is so deeply buried that I will not be able to dig it out when it is needed." He made a savage scooping motion with two fingers. "Like I long to dig out the hearts of the Buffalo Soldiers, and watch their fort burn to the ground."

"All of this is foretold," Springs of Life said, soothingly. He watched the old man next to him become calm. The fire in his eyes still burned, but deeply, which was good. Pretorio had spent too much time lately on outward anger. It was the inner anger they needed for victory, the memories of his brother Victorio's defeat, and the victory that would soon be theirs. "They will fight," Springs of Life said, proudly.

Pretorio grunted. "And what of our two scouts?"

Springs of Life hesitated before answering. One of them had been his own grandson, the other the grandson of his dead brother. "I fear something has happened to them."

"Oh?" Pretorio taunted. "And have they not run like jackrabbits, never to be caught?"

"As I told you when Waiting Moon failed to return, there is a small, strange medicine in the far mountains, something that is eating at the Buffalo Soldiers, too—"

"I am sick of your strange medicines!" Pretorio said testily. "You make excuses for these pups. They should not have been sent, dressed as *Lipan.*" He spit on the ground. "You might well have dressed them as women. This is what the Lipan have become . . ."

"But with your leadership, the Lipan will join us, and we will make one great nation."

Pretorio straightened in his saddle. "This is so. I should not speak so harshly of our brothers. It is just that, they have lived so long among the white eyes, that they have become like the white eyes."

Pretorio and his medicine man stood watching the caravan below them for a few moments.

Carefully, thinking again of his grandson and the grandson of his brother, Springs of Life said, "Perhaps we should send two more scouts . . ."

Pretorio grunted. "Let it be so." He turned to smile grimly. "If we are warriors, we can still worry for our own, can we not?"

"And you will soon achieve your vengeance," Springs of Life added quietly.

"This is right," Pretorio said. Springs of Life watched his companion rub involuntarily at a spot below his neck. Five years before, a Buffalo Soldier bullet had entered Pretorio's son's neck at the same spot, killing him.

"And—" Springs of Life began.

"And," Pretorio said, "I will kill, with my own hands, the Buffalo Soldier named Thomas Mullin."

# *Chapter Sixteen*

Lincoln Reeves awoke in a shaded place. A dull ache greeted him when he moved his head. His right eye was swollen nearly shut.

He seemed to be in a cave. A line of bright sunlight cut the far wall; on peering at it, Lincoln saw what looked like a turn in the cave wall. Apparently, he was angled around a corner, in the cool rear of a mountain cutout.

More slowly this time, he turned his head, in the other direction.

A figure was huddled not five feet from him, face to the cave wall. It was curled up like a baby. Lincoln could see nothing of the face, but the clothes were torn and dirty. A pair of scuffed boots lay nearby.

Lincoln tried his bonds. The man who had tied them this time wasn't drunk; they were tight and secure, feet and hands bound separately, hands behind. He moved his hands, searching for a sharp rock to rub the rope against.

At that moment, the figure sat up and looked at him.

Not at him, exactly. The young man had a horrible sunburn, deep red patches of skin flaking from his face and hands. His thin hair had been bleached nearly white. His lips were cracked and swollen.

His eyes were very wide, looked forced open. The young man peered to the side, averting his vision.

Still, Lincoln had the uncomfortable feeling the man was staring straight at him.

"Awake?" the young man said.

"Yes."

The young man tittered, showed small, yellowed teeth behind his dried lips. "Good. It will be dark soon."

"I don't think—"

"Are you hungry? I should ask my army—do you eat?"

"I . . . yes, I'm hungry."

Lincoln noticed now the empty feeling in his belly.

"Good. I will let you eat with me."

The young man pulled on his boots and scrabbled away, stopping a moment at the far end of the turnout to stare out past the bright light, smiling, then disappeared around the corner wall and was gone from the cave.

Lincoln resumed looking for a sharp rock, finding one behind him on the wall, and began to scrape away at the rope binding his hands.

There was dried beef, and water, which the young man fed to Lincoln. The light on the far wall had dropped in height and intensity, signalling the coming of twilight.

"I have saved food, from the many saddlebags," the young man explained, and, from the way the young man looked at him, with his faced cocked to the side, and smiling, Lincoln thought the young man assumed he knew what he was talking about.

Lincoln nodded.

"You will make a good army for me. Are there many in the Army of the Night?"

Lincoln looked at the young man blankly.

The young man leaned forward, instantly angry. There was a sliver of dried beef in his hand, which he dashed to the ground. "One thing there must be in an army is discipline. I love you, because you are mine, but you must obey me." The young man produced a long knife, cut out with it.

Lincoln gasped, falling back; a hot line cut across his cheek.

The young man dropped the knife, sprang forward, tore a thin rag from his shirt and dabbed at the cut.

"You must believe me," he said sincerely. He seemed on the verge of weeping. "That was not something I wanted to do." He leaned back, studied the strip of cloth with his averted vision. "The cut was not deep. Now. Are there many in the Army of the Night?"

Lincoln hesitated, said, "Yes."

"Good! And are all of them at the fort ready to serve me?"

Lincoln studied the man's face, saw quick anger rising again. "Of course."

"Good!" He seemed about to dance, rocking up on his heels. "Then you, my General, must get them for me. Tell them it is our time. The Sun is dead. Do you understand?"

Lincoln said, "Yes."

The young man darted forward, the knife again in hand. Lincoln flinched back, but the young man made two quick cuts, through the bindings on his feet and then around back, cutting the rope tying his hands. The young man stepped back, held the knife in front of him, moving his eyes from side to side, studying Lincoln while he rose.

"Tell them," the young man said, "that I will be in the mountains, waiting. I will watch them come down to me, from on high. You will do that?"

Lincoln stood stiffly, rubbing at his wrists. "I will," he said.

The young man laughed, went into the far corner, gathered dried beef into a satchel and produced a canteen, filled with water. He handed them to Lincoln. "Come with me!"

Lincoln followed the young man to the turn in the cave wall. There was a short ledge, and then they were standing outside, on the lip of a mountain. Below them, a hillock-dotted plain, which Lincoln took to be Limpia Canyon near Wild Rose Pass, stretched as far as sight. The evening was beautiful, low tufts of cloud reflecting the orange glory of the setting sun.

The young man was staring straight into the dropping Sun, eyes unblinking. He did not avert his vision. Lincoln thought of a story he had heard about a trooper staked out in the sun by Apaches whose eyelids had been cut off. He had suffered retinal blindness, which darkened the center of vision but left sight at the edges.

The young man laughed, then sighed, almost tenderly. Lincoln felt a brief touch on his arm.

"All of this," the young man said, "will be ours!"

Using his own averted vision, Lincoln saw that the young man stood just far enough away from him to be dangerous, and that the knife was still held tightly in one hand.

"Are you ready?" the young man said.

"Yes."

The young man suddenly tittered. "Good! I have one more task for you before you go." Still laughing, he darted back into the cave. Briefly, Lincoln thought of flight. But the young man reappeared almost immediately, bearing a saddlebag, which he dug into.

"Here!"

Lincoln held out his hand.

The young man made to place something in it, then held back. Again, Lincoln felt a light touch on his arm.

"First," the young man said, "I will tell you that those who have sought to hurt my general are in my sight. If you obey, no harm can come to you. You will be avenged."

Suddenly the young man laughed again, put something down into Lincoln's hand. Lincoln looked down to see a pouch, a small square of paper.

The young man laughed loudly, slapped Lincoln on the back.

"Make me a cigarette!" he said.

# *Chapter Seventeen*

It was late afternoon before Porter was willing to admit they were lost. The arguments had started almost immediately that morning, with whether they should bury Captain Murphy or bring his body back. Porter had finally won out, arguing that if they brought the captain back there was a chance the surgeon at Fort Davis could figure out how he died. "If we bury him out here," Porter had said, "and not too well, there's a chance that by the time anybody gets to him, since we won't be able to remember where we put him anyway, that there'll be nothing but buzzard-eaten bones left. And bones don't tell stories."

Chaney had nodded, but Sommers was still skeptical. "You think there won't be an inquiry? If the Army doesn't do it, Pinkerton himself will. You know what the old Scot bastard is like—and he knew Murphy."

"Last I heard, Pinkerton was at death's door. And Smith in St. Louis I can handle." Porter grinned. "And anyway, Sommers, I'm in charge. I'd hate to have to explain another death."

Sommers broke eye contact with Porter. "All right," he said.

The arguments hadn't ended there, though. After burying Murphy badly, in a shallow pit covered with just enough dirt so that the coyotes and mountain lions would have no trouble unburying him, they loaded up and set out, Porter in front.

"Porter," said Sommers, cautiously, after an hour of riding through rough hills, "you know where you're taking us? Shouldn't we get back to Limpia Creek, follow that back down to the fort?"

"I know what I'm doing," Porter said. He gave Sommers a harsh look. "If we follow that creek, we're liable to meet that darkie Mullin, or Captain Seavers' boys coming out from Fort Davis. Last thing we need is to find somebody now, and have to do a lot of explaining before we're ready. We'll just follow the line of the creek up in the hills here, off the canyon."

"Looks like we're getting too far west. I remember the line of these hills coming in—"

Porter's voice was ice. "I don't want to have to tell you again, Sommers. I'm in charge."

Sommers tried to lock eyes with Porter again, failed.

"Let's go," Porter said. He took his flask from his pocket, tilted a short shot into his mouth, replaced the flask. Then, spurring his horse, he led farther up into the hills, away from Limpia Canyon.

In late afternoon, Porter brought them to a halt. "We'll bed down here for the night." He had his flask out again, emptying it. He reached back to his saddlebag for the bottle there. "Tomorrow," he said, his voice showing signs of alcohol consumption, "we'll head back to the creek, ride into the fort. Doesn't matter if we meet anyone after this; we couldn't lead them back to Murphy if we tried."

Chaney was already down, pulling his pack from his mount. Sommers eyed Porter a moment, then followed suit.

Darkness found them all drunk. Sommers and Chaney played cards solemnly, nursing their own bottle, while Porter sat off, nearly beyond the light of the fire, quietly emptying his own.

"You know," Porter said, out of the darkness, his words slurred, "killing ain't so hard."

Chaney started to look up, but Sommers held his arm. "Just

deal," he said quietly. Chaney shrugged, turned another card and looked at the result.

"No," Porter said, his voice rising. "I thought it would be hard, but it wasn't."

Now Chaney did look up. "Thought you said you killed lots of times."

Porter's face, indistinct, snapped up. "What?"

"I said," Chaney repeated, "I thought you killed a lot of times. That's what you told us."

Porter made a growling sound, waved the bottle at them drunkenly. "Whatever I said. Sure." He waved the bottle again, brought it to his mouth, drank. The bottle slipped from his hands, fell to the ground.

Again Porter made a growling sound. He tried to find the bottle, could not locate it in the near dark. He lay down, made a short laughing sound. "Just a darkie, anyway," he said.

When Sommers looked over, Porter was snoring, on his back, the bottle a few inches from his outstretched hand.

Sommers watched Porter for a few moments. "Three more deals," he said to Chaney, "then we tie him up."

Chaney's face peered at him. "Why?"

"Because he's gonna kill us, or get us killed. We'll tell our own story when we get into Fort Davis. Man like Porter, sooner or later he'll slip. Then the three of us hang. If we tell what happened, he'll hang alone. We'll tell them he threatened to kill us if we didn't follow him. That's not far from true."

Chaney considered briefly. "All right," he said.

"Deal," Sommers said.

They played three more hands. Porter, on his back, made a gurgling sound, then was silent.

Sommers signalled, and Chaney put the cards down. Sommers got a length of rope from his pack, and the two men approached Porter.

"Turn him over, carefully," Sommers said. He stood back a pace, hand to his gun. "Don't wake him up."

Chaney squatted, took Porter by the arm and opposite shoulder, started to turn him over.

"Jumpin' blazes," Chaney said, standing up quickly.

"What is it?"

Chaney held his hand up, drenched in blood.

"What the—" Sommers said. He bent down, angled so that the weak firelight illuminated Porter's face.

"His throat's been cut."

"How—" Chaney began.

"Be quiet!" Sommers hissed. He had his hand to his gun, fumbled it out of its holster. He paced back toward the fire, Chaney following.

"I still don't—" Chaney said.

"There's somebody here!" Sommers said, fear in his voice. "Indians, or that killer—"

A shape flashed out of the dark, covered Chaney briefly. Sommers saw a glint of straight steel, saw Chaney try to raise his arm, then scream out. The figure jumped away, back into the darkness, leaving Chaney falling to the ground, front washed in blood.

Chaney made a bubbling sound in his cut throat, then stared at Sommers, eyes dead and glazed.

"Holy hell," Sommers said. He backed nearly into the fire, stopped. A slight sound behind him and he turned, gun raised. The campfire spat sparks in front of him, blinding him.

"Holy living hell."

There was a tittering sound, to his left.

He jumped, shot wildly that way.

The laughter came from behind him.

"You have harmed a soldier of my army," a voice giggled. The voice faded as it spoke. Now Sommers heard laughter off to his right.

"Who are you! Let's talk!"

"You hurt my soldier."

Again Sommers twisted around, hearing the voice behind him. "It wasn't me! It was Porter, the man whose throat you cut!"

"Yours is the throat I cut!"

A shape ran at him. Sommers got the gun halfway up. The shape flashed past. He felt a nick below his chin, felt brief warmth, reached up to pat a dot of blood from a shallow cut.

He felt the figure circling him, drew his gun up.

The shape came at him from the back; again he felt a nick below his chin.

"Now I'm coming!" the voice in the night laughed.

"No!"

Sommers fired his gun wildly, left and right, and ran.

Something loomed on the ground and Sommers screamed, tripping over it. It was Porter's body.

Sommers pushed himself to his feet and ran on. He was in a darkness, clothed in bright stars. There was a moon rising in the distance. He ran blindly toward it, tripping over stones, righting himself. He twisted around and fired again.

"No!"

He turned to run on, but the moon was gone. Then, suddenly, it reappeared, uneclipsed by the head of a human form directly in his path. As Sommers stumbled into the shape, the moon hung above it, like a crescent crown.

"I told you I was coming," the figure said, arms stretched out in welcome, one hand holding straight the blade that sank deep and true into Sommers' throat.

# *Chapter Eighteen*

Adams knew all along what Seavers would do. He had known it the moment that the Captain decided he would lead the expedition to find, capture, or disband the renegade Mescaleros heading for Fort Davis.

The only problem was time. Adams had calculated that Seavers' insistence on heading south and then west would cost them one day, perhaps two. By that time, if the Mescaleros cut straight across from the Eagle Mountains, the way Thomas had thought they would, there was a chance Seavers would miss them completely and the renegade Apaches could drop in on a relatively unprotected fort. With most of the Tenth Cavalry out in the mountains, the fort, along with the mostly white and inexperienced officer corps led by that idiot Forsen, might easily fall. And then there would be real hell to pay.

Seavers' game was obvious: follow Thomas Mullin's plan but pretend it was his own. Thus the initial southward heading. The Captain could pretend to be following some calculation of his own; when he did abruptly turn westward, it would look original and brilliant.

Adams eyed the surrounding hills and thought of Custer at Little

Big Horn. The hills there had been similar, and had been proven decisive to Custer's defeat. Seavers' cultivated physical appearance was so close to Custer's that Adams feared his mental makeup was the same.

Why do I feel like Bentine? he thought, thinking of Custer's doomed second in command.

He pulled up alongside the Captain and said, "Sir, I think we ought to send a patrol out now. If you could give me three men—"

"I was about to suggest you take *one* man, Lieutenant," Seavers said, without turning to look at Adams.

"Very good, Sir," Adams said, saluting, turning back into the troop.

"Sergeant Chase, come with me," he said, signalling out one of the few men he could trust.

Chase saluted smartly and pulled his mount out.

The two men kicked their horses and sped off. In another few minutes, they had left Seavers' troops a half mile and one low hill behind.

"You can slow it down now, he can't hear us," Adams said dryly.

"Lieutenant," Chase said, "what in hell is the Captain trying to do?"

Adams shook his head, looking straight ahead, studying the mass of hills around them. "He's trying to be George Armstrong Custer," Adams said, "and I'm afraid he's going to get the same end result."

Without another word, Adams kicked his horse and pulled off, Chase following close behind.

They spent the rest of the day doing a large circle around Seavers' troop, making sure there was no immediate danger. Adams thought the Mescaleros would be at least two days away, but they might have sent an advance party out to scout the hills. Word that a troop from Fort Davis was wandering the hills between the Davis and Eagle mountains would surely be welcome in the Mescalero camp. If Thomas was right, and Pretorio was indeed leading the renegade band, the Mescaleros would go straight for the troop. And if there were two hundred of them, like Thomas estimated . . .

"Let's head northwest of here, up where Seavers should have gone," Adams said, an hour before sunset. "We'll have to do a little night riding, if you don't mind. We can bed down later, west of Cherry Canyon. I've got a feeling . . ."

"I've got the same feeling, Lieutenant," Chase said. After a moment he added, "I made a big decision today."

"What's that, Sergeant?" Adams asked.

"I was eligible to bring my wife out to the fort," Chase said. "There's no way in hell I'll do it with that madman Seavers in command."

"You made the right decision, Sergeant," Adams said.

The two men kicked their horses, heading north of the sunset.

Around midnight, Adams and Chase ended their ride. Forgoing a fire, they ate cold rations on a ridge with a western view.

Adams indicated a spot just to the east of a mountain called Sawtooth. "What I've got in mind is, they'll pass right down through there. We don't patrol it much, and it's easy passage. They'll be bringing their squaus and children with them, probably a wagon or two if they've got it. Even if they're on foot and horseback, it's the easiest pass in this area. From there they could just fly through all the canyons, Medera and Little Aguja, down under Black Mountain, around Flat Top and down on the fort. Meanwhile, that idiot Seavers will be down around Barrel Springs. Even if he cuts west tomorrow, he'd miss them."

"The way he was talking," Chase said, "it sounded like he thought he'd circle around and catch them from behind, pinch them between the fort and himself."

"That's not what he thought at all," Adams said, angrily. "If he did, he'd have at least a half a thought in his head. Mullin would have told him to do that if he thought Seaver would leave right away. The only way to get them from behind is to cut real close to them."

"Then Seavers is just plain stupid," Chase said.

Adams smiled, rose, went to his bedroll and lay down. "I knew there was hope for you, son. Wake me in four hours."

Chase woke Adams three hours later. Adams sat up, feeling Chase's tension, and immediately knew why.

A shrill bird's whistle echoed below and to the west of them; another answered from the east.

"That's not very far away," Adams whispered. He gripped Chase's arm, pulled his ear close. "Stay here, and keep the horses quiet."

"But Lieutenant—"

Adams gripped harder. "Do what I say. I might be gone a long time. Just hold on. If you hear me holler, get on your horse and ride the hell back to Seavers, fast as you can." Adams turned Chase's face to his so the young man could see his seriousness. "You hear me, son?"

"Yes, Sir."

Adams crawled away from Chase, into the dark, down over the lip of their ridge.

Chase listened for a sound, but heard none, until, a little while later, the far whistle came, answered by its mate.

The night was interminably long. Chase kept his ears cocked, but heard only one further whistle. There was no wind. The stars were silent, and the moon, in crescent phase, came up late and shed no light on the plains below.

Deep in the night, toward morning, Chase heard what he thought was a distant shout, but he couldn't be sure. A half hour later he had convinced himself that it had indeed been Adams when he heard a scrabble of rocks below.

He pulled his sidearm, peered into darkness.

A head appeared over the lip of the ridge. Chase aimed his gun, held it on the figure.

"For God's sake, Chase, give me a hand!"

Chase holstered his pistol and ran to the Lieutenant. Adams was breathing heavily, favoring his left leg.

"Are you all right, Lieutenant?"

"The hell with me," Adams said. He pressed his thigh, grimaced. "It was my own fault. Quick, get those horses ready to go. We've got a fast ride."

"What—"

"I'll tell you while we ride, dammit!"

"Yes, Sir."

Chase rolled their packs, broke camp. In a few minutes he was helping Adams up onto his mount. The Lieutenant made a gasping sound as he sat upright, left hand holding his leg, right hand holding the reins.

"Let's go, Sergeant."

They rode down off the ridge. When they had reached the plain below, Adams pulled alongside the Sergeant.

"Sir, what the hell is going on?"

"I'll tell it to you quick," Adams said. With each of the horse's strides, Adams grimaced. "There were two of them. I caught the first one as he was bedding down. He was Mescalero, up and down. The other was a mile away, but he was ready because the first hadn't answered his final whistle. I jumped too soon, hit a rock. He didn't even try to fight, just got onto his horse and rode. I figure the rest are twenty miles behind. If we hadn't come up here they would have hit the fort unmolested. The bad news is, now they think the whole bunch of us are already nearby, and they'll head south." Adams grimaced, his face grim. Chase spurred his own horse to keep up. "That means, when Seavers heads northwest, he'll run straight into their arms. And in those hills, if we don't find Seavers today, we'll have another real George Custer on our hands."

# Chapter Nineteen

Thomas watched the distant figure for a long time before he had an inkling of who it was. Even then he was not sure; he had ridden most of the night, and his eyes were tired, and he was more than frustrated at not finding the Pinkerton men and Reeves.

But then he was sure. The train of logic in his tired mind hooked up its cars, and he saw the pattern laid out in front of him. He would have done the same thing, had he been in this spot.

He brought his horse down quickly from the rise, spurred it toward the figure which even now was weaving with each step in the bright afternoon sun.

"Lincoln!" Thomas shouted, hailing the walking figure.

Trooper Reeves stood straight, stared, raised a hand in salute, and then promptly collapsed.

Thomas reached the young soldier, dismounted, lifted Lincoln's head from the ground.

Reeves looked up weakly. "Been walking since last night. Thought . . . you'd be by."

"You did well, son," Thomas said. "Now we'll get you out of this heat." Mullin began to lift the young man onto his horse.

"Lieutenant?" Reeves said weakly.

"What is it?"

Reeves smiled wanly. "Teach me how to read, will you? I want to follow that Sherlock Holmes."

"You already have, son," Mullin said. "You've already used your head."

After an hour out of the sun, after judiciously rationed water, Reeves was ready to talk.

"There's things I've got to tell you, Sir," Reeves said. "You won't believe—"

"All right if I guess? "Thomas said.

"You mean, like Sherlock Holmes?"

Thomas found that he couldn't deny the charge. "It's vain of me, I know—"

"Go ahead, Sir."

"Well," Thomas said, "to begin with, there was trouble with the Pinkerton men. I'd say it had something to do with you being Negro. I"—Thomas hesitated.—"noticed the rope marks around your neck."

"They tried to hang me," Reeves said.

"From the rips on your clothing in the back, I figure they had a horse drag you. Your hands and feet were bound. Thing I can't figure is, what were you doing so far north? You said yourself, you walked all night. That means your horse got away from you."

Reeves was bursting with excitement. "He found me."

"Who?"

"The killer. The one you figured killed the Senator's son, all those other people."

"What!"

"It's true, Lieutenant. It had to be him. The Pinkerton's head man died from exposure and alcohol poisoning. Porter, who more or less ran things anyway, got drunk, and the other two couldn't stop him from hanging me. I got loose, walked a ways, until I couldn't walk anymore. When I collapsed there was someone there, standing over me. I thought for sure it was Porter. It wasn't. The man standing over me said some strange things, asked me some questions. He had a knife out at one point, and I thought for sure he was going to kill me.

"I blacked out, thought I was dead for sure. When I woke up, I was in a cave. I'm pretty sure it was in the side of Star Mountain. He'd brought me there, carried me on his back. He's young, maybe twenty, twenty-one. He's white, but he has a horrible sunburn. I think he burned part of his eyes out. He kept looking at me out of the sides of his eyes. Also, he stares at the sun all the time. He was creepy as hell, Lieutenant."

"He let you go?" Thomas said.

"I didn't even have a chance to try to get away on my own. He kept talking nonsense, about the Army of the Night, how I was his general. He's crazy as a rabid dog. He handed me a pouch and cigarette paper, told me to make him a cigarette. Then he gave me a little to eat and drink from some saddlebags he had stored up there and told me to go. He said he'd be watching from above, that I was to get the rest of the Army of the Night."

"I'll be damned." Thomas considered for a moment. "Did he say anything else strange, Trooper?"

"Everything he said was strange, Sir. He was mighty happy when he found that I was a Negro. He was going to kill me until then, I'm sure."

"What do you mean?"

"The first thing I remember him saying was, 'Are you more than seventeen?' Then he gasped, and took hold of my cheek, then started all that stuff about the Army of the Night. There's another thing you'll find interesting, Sir."

"Yes?"

"In the Valley below Star Mountain, at the bottom of the trail leading down, I found another one of those circles, like the grave we found the Indian in. It looked new."

Thomas was nodding his head thoughtfully.

"He also said another thing I've been thinking about. He said not to worry, that those who sought to harm me were in his sight. I figure he was talking about the Pinkertons."

Thomas continued to nod. "Trooper, do you have with you . . ."

"Yes, Sir." Reeves reached into his shirt, produced a bundle of papers and handed them over. "The information you requested, Sir." Suddenly, his story told, Reeves was very tired.

Thomas opened them immediately. "Relax, Trooper," he said. "I can't tell you how helpful you've been."

"I am kind of tired, Sir," Reeves said.

"Sleep, now. I'll wake you later. We've got some work ahead of us, but you'll be no use if you're exhausted."

"Yes, sir."

Reeves lay down, watched the older man turn away, eyes peering closely over the papers, hunched over like a scholar.

Reeves awoke refreshed. His body ached, but it was a good ache, tired and hurt muscles gaining the rest they need, ready to work again.

Thomas was still hunched over; there was another paper spread out next to the ones Lincoln had given him, and Thomas was turning his attention from one to the other, marking one paper and then the other.

"I trust you feel better, Trooper?" Thomas said, without taking his attention away from the work in front of him.

"Yes, Sir," Lincoln said. He rose, stretched, noted that the sun had angled toward late afternoon.

"You slept five hours," Thomas said. "It will have to do, because we have an all night ride ahead of us."

"That's fine with me, Sir."

"We have a stop to make before it gets dark. I want to visit that cave in the side of Star Mountain."

"You think he'll still be there?"

Thomas looked up briefly, went back to his work. "No, he won't be there. I want to visit the grave."

"You think it's the Senator's son?"

"I know it's the Senator's son."

"How . . ."

"Come here, Trooper," Thomas said.

Reeves approached, sat down beside Thomas. The older man pointed to the second paper, which was a map of the Davis Mountain area.

"You see this circle?" Thomas said, tracing the drawn arc, marked with numbered *X*'s, around the circumference of the mountain area.

"Looks like the circle of the graves," Lincoln said, indicating the bulge at the circle's western edge, on Flat Top Mountain.

"It's the same thing," Mullin said. "The *X*'s are gravesites. Can you read numbers?"

"A little, Sir."

Mullin pulled the paper Reeves had delivered over so that Reeves could see it. Many of the entries on the paper were marked with numbers. "These numbers correspond with the numbered gravesites. Every one of the disappearances I marked on this paper happened in an area near this circle. Three of these graves I've found already. I'd be willing to bet we find the rest of them just about where I have them marked on this map." He pointed to a particular one, marked 23, on Star Mountain. "There's the Senator's son."

"My Lord," Lincoln said. "He killed all those people . . ."

"He's been at it for more than two years. A settler here, a rancher there, stragglers, cowboys, campers. Anyone who met his preconditions, namely, that they be more than seventeen years old. Only he knows why. There are a lot of people in this area, most of them unconnected to anyone else. Nobody ever bothered to look for a pattern."

Reeves was still staring at the map in wonder.

"He's killed at least twenty-seven people. That includes the Pinkertons, who I'm sure are dead."

"You really think . . . ?"

"I'm sure of it, Trooper. This man killed your assailants, just as surely as he killed that Mescalero scout and the other twenty-three people I have marked on this map. And unless we go to the place he is now, and capture or kill him, he will continue to slaughter anyone who falls into his web and happens to fit his conditions."

"But where . . . ?"

Mullin could not help showing his pride. It was a trait, he told himself, even if a bad one, he shared with Sherlock Holmes. "Oh, I know exactly where to find him, where he is at this very moment. That's why I suggest we stop talking, and ride."

Already, Reeves had begun to break camp.

A three hour ride, which used most of the rest of the day, brought them to the plain at the foot of Star Mountain, and the fresh, circular grave dug there.

Reeves eyed the shallow cave set into the side of the mountain, a hundred feet above them. "Sure he's not up there, Lieutenant?"

"He's not," Mullins answered shortly. He had begun to dig. "I think you should go up while I examine the grave and find whatever evidence you can, though. Believe me, Trooper, he's long gone." He looked up at Reeves, smiled wryly. "You don't believe me?" He took out his sidearm, handed it to the private. "Take this. Shoot at shadows if you want."

"Thank you, Sir."

Reeves climbed cautiously, the handgun out. The climb took only twenty minutes. When he reached the ledge leading to the cave a chill went through him.

He found the remains of a rolled cigarette and little more. Two saddlebags inside the mouth of the cave held a little dried beef, a boy's pocketknife, a tattered book with a drawing of the moon on the cover. Inside were drawings of the constellations, the lines between stars carefully drawn in by hand. On the flyleaf of the book, written in a tight, sharp hand, was an inscription.

Lincoln climbed down the slope, book in hand. Thomas Mullin was standing solemnly by the dug-up circle of the grave.

"Say hello to Robert Loggins, son of Senator Will Loggins of Missouri," Mullin said.

Reeves quietly regarded the uncovered skull, bits of dried skin still adhered to it. The jaw had been opened, showing a festering, drying mass of entrails inside.

"The lower teeth are all we needed for identification," Thomas said. "They match exactly the description I was given, down to the missing right bicuspid." Mullin sighed. "We've done our work, Trooper."

"I found this up in the cave," Reeves said, handing Thomas the book.

The Lieutenant studied the book, turned it over in his hands, looked at the drawn constellations within, opened to the flyleaf. He read the inscription aloud: *"For Curtis, from the staff of Griffith Observatory, Chicago."* Suddenly he gave a whoop of exultation. "You make one hell of a good Watson, Reeves," he said.

"Sir?"

"You must excuse my blunder, son. It was stupid of me not to want to study that cave immediately myself. I should have remembered my Sherlock Holmes. Just because the man wasn't here, doesn't mean he didn't leave himself behind."

Reeves still looked puzzled.

Mullin flipped through the book, stopped at a marked page. On it was a list of symbols. One of them, a circle with a cross at its perimeter, was marked.

"The symbol for the planet Venus," Thomas read. "It's also the symbol for Woman."

Thomas fumbled the map and other papers out of his pocket. He looked briefly at the map, then stabbed his finger at the list of names.

"That's him," he said to Reeves. "That's the killer."

Reeves saw the name, heard Thomas say it: "Curtis Marks."

"The killer's name is Curtis Marks?"

"Not much of a name for a man who's murdered so many, is it? He must be"—Thomas studied the short entry—"twenty years old now. This explains almost everything." He looked up at Lincoln, eyes bright. "The mystery is solved, Trooper Reeves. I not only know where the killer is, but who he is, why he kills and why we'll find him where he is now."

Reeves tried to understand, managed only a blank look.

"Read, boy! Read!"

Reeves stood mute, and Thomas said, "Of course, I forgot. We'll do something about that when we have time." His triumphant look returned. "This disappearance occurred two and a half years ago. I thought it was the first one, originally. Now I see my mistake. It clears so much up." Mullin's eyes glowed with excitement. "Curtis Marks got off a train in Abilene, headed out to Arizona Territory from Chicago. According to this, he was AWOL from the Army at the time. I'm sure he had a strange service record. He never got back on the train. He must have had an . . . interesting childhood."

Reeves waited for Thomas to continue.

"Curtis Marks," Thomas said slowly, "came out west, and got off that train in Abilene, with his mother."

# Chapter Twenty

Captain Seavers thought a lot now about his career. With luck, this action against the Mescaleros could gain for him the two things he wanted more fervently than he had ever wanted anything in his life: to get out of Fort Davis—and with the rank of General.

It was not unlikely. After all, that was the only thing that made you in this army anymore, the attainment of high rank coupled with service against the Indians. Seavers still felt the sharp jab of furious disappointment he had felt the year before when assignment to Fort Davis had come. Everyone knew it was a dead-end job. The Indian Wars in Texas were four years over. Fort Davis and its Tenth Cavalry were at the very bottom in fort assignments. The glory days in west Texas were gone, and any man sent to command this desert post with its band of misfit officers and . . . well, Negro soldiers, was more or less not a man marked by destiny for greatness.

But greatness, Seavers had always believed, was something that could just as well be manufactured as won, and here was his chance to do it. Grierson and his bunch had thought they had tamed this part of the country for good when Victorio was defeated, but now Seavers would be the man who took care of west Texas for all time.

After he had not only driven back, but annihilated, this rogue band of Mescaleros, a plum post, and promotion, could not be far behind. Destiny would be his, after all.

It bothered him a little that Adams had not agreed wholeheartedly with his plan, because, even though Adams was a troublemaker and, nearly unique among his men, a fraternizer with the Negro troops, Seavers had always found him to be a good man in the field. And, God knew, he needed more of them. He almost chided himself on getting rid of the man by sending him out on patrol, but decided that it had been a good move after all, because Adam's dissention here in the ranks would have done more harm than good.

Seavers still felt sure of his plan. They had turned north just after camping down the night before, and now, with luck, would reach the middle of Little Aguja Canyon by afternoon. So far, his scout had seen no Mescaleros. If Adams had not already located them, it would be easy enough work to do so, and act accordingly. With luck, the whole operation would be over today, and he could get back to his office and begin to write that report that would get him out of this hell hole. And get back to drinking coffee at his desk . . .

"Another cup, Sir?" the cook, Rivers, asked. Rivers could not keep the belligerent tone that Seavers so disliked about many of the Negroes out of his voice.

"Yes, another cup, please. And then tell Trooper Franklin to get the men to mount up."

Rivers bowed slightly, managed to make it a sarcastic motion. "Yes, Sir."

Seavers swivelled in his camp stool, watched the retreating Negro, made a note to remember to have him transferred when they got back to the fort. He took another swallow of coffee, gagged, spit it out and emptied the rest out of the china cup onto the ground. He put the cup down on his silver service, set up on his map table.

"Rivers!" he shouted.

The cook, twenty paces away, turned and looked at him questioningly. "Sir?"

"Get back here!"

Rivers came back quickly.

"Stand at attention!" Seavers shouted.

Rivers stood straight. "Yes, Sir."

Seavers pointed with anger to his empty coffee cup. "What kind of coffee was that?"

"Chicory coffee, Sir."

"What!"

"I'm sorry, Sir. I should have told the Captain that his store of regular coffee was depleted. I thought the Captain understood that all we had left was chicory coffee." Rivers looked at Seavers imploringly. "Sir."

Seavers' voice rose menacingly. "Did I, or did I not, tell you to bring sufficient regular coffee for a week in the field?"

Rivers, at rigid attention, said, "You did, Sir."

"Then what in blue hell happened to it!"

"I . . . must have miscalculated, Sir."

"Did you miscalculate, or did you deliberately hold back? Did you, by any chance, give extra regular coffee to Thomas Mullin?"

Rivers swallowed hard and said, "Some may have slipped into his pack, Sir."

"How much?"

Rivers shriveled under Seavers's glare. "A week's worth, Sir. I truly had no idea—"

"And did he willingly take it?"

"I wouldn't put it that way, Sir—"

"Rivers," Seavers said, with frightening cool anger, "think very carefully. Your career will depend on your answer, and if you spend the next month, or the next year, in stockade. Here is my question: did Mr. Mullin, a civilian, willingly accept coffee, U.S. Army property which he knows to be in short supply, and which he specifically knows, being a former officer of the

United States Army, that, being in short supply, is subject to hording laws?"

Rivers broke his attention, again looked to Seavers for mercy. "Sir, please—"

"Stand at attention, damn you!"

Rivers snapped to attention. "Begging your pardon, Sir," Rivers said, swallowing hard, "but I cannot answer that question."

"Cannot! Or *will* not!"

"Sir—"

Captain Seavers turned from Rivers with a snort of disgust. There was dead silence. The rest of the troop had stopped to watch his tirade in mute witness.

"The whole bunch of you," Seavers shouted, "disgust me! This isn't a command, it's a playpen!" Livid with anger, Seavers raised his fist, beat it down in frustration against his palm. "I don't belong here! Do you realize the Tenth Cavalry has had thirty commanding officers in the last fifteen years? Do you realize I've spent the last twelve months with the worst sanitation, the worst supplies, the worst communications and the worst command in all of the United States Army? Do you know why my wife sits back at home in Baltimore, alone? Because I wouldn't dare subject her to this! She would not be proud of me! I am not proud of myself!" Seavers turned slowly, taking in the sea of solemn black faces surrounding him. "The Indians," he said, sarcastically, "call you Buffalo Soldiers—and you wear it as a badge of pride! The Army puts you in the hell hole of the country—and you hold your heads high, and call yourselves soldiers, and make believe you are worthy! Stand at attention dammit—all of you!"

As one, the troop went to rigid attention.

"Well," Seavers said, "you are well-trained fools, nevertheless. And I have every intention—"

A single gunshot sounded in the distance. Seavers looked up to see a horse approaching fast from the north, kicking dust. As it got closer he saw that there were two riders, one of them slumped behind the other. The front rider was driving the horse, whipping the reins from side to side.

The troop moved aside as the horse galloped into camp, pulled up short in front of Captain Seavers. Sergeant Chase, covered in dust, breathing heavily, saluted and said, "Sergeant Chase and Lieutenant Adams reporting, Sir—"

"The hell with that," Adams said. He was clinging weakly to Chase's back, barely conscious. When he moved to straighten up he gave a gasp of pain, grit his teeth. He turned his eyes on Seavers, stared hard. "Congratulations, Captain."

Seavers' anger began to return. "I will not be spoken to—"

Adams grinned weakly. "You got what you wanted. I see you camped right inside the mouth of Little Aguja Canyon. If you hadn't, we would have been able to warn you in time. In my wildest dreams, I didn't think you were that stupid . . ."

Seavers was livid. "How dare—"

"Doesn't matter," Adams said, barely a whisper. His eyes went glassy. "I feel more and more like Bentine . . ."

Adams collapsed, slid down from the horse where two troopers supported him and lowered him to the ground.

Still red with rage, Seavers turned to Chase. "What in hell is going on here!"

Chase saluted. "Mescaleros, Sir. We found your scout four miles north of here, dead. The Indians must have come in during the night. They're all around you, Sir, up on the ridges."

"That's ridiculous," Seavers began.

As if in answer, a rifle shot went off above.

A growing line of Apaches snugged the tops of the surrounding hills. A double rank of Mescaleros was closing off the mouth of Little Aguja Canyon behind them. At their head a chief raised his rifle in signal, fired a shot, kicked his horse forward.

The whoop of war cries rose.

"Deploy!" Captain Seavers shouted.

Already, the troop was moving into circular formation, overturning wagons, grounding their horses. Seavers ran for his tent to retrieve his sidearm, knocked into his map table, upsetting his silver service, knocking his coffee pot to the ground.

Chase dismounted, dragged Lieutenant Adams to the shelter of an ammunition wagon. In its shade, Adams regained consciousness, heard the commotion around him, smiled grimly up at Chase.

"Welcome to Little Big Horn," he said.

# *Chapter Twenty-One*

Thomas Mullin and Lincoln Reeves heard the battle from a distance as a strange whooping echo rising and falling through the hills.

"What—" Reeves said.

Thomas didn't have to be told what he was hearing. Though he hadn't heard it in years, the sound was all too familiar to him. And still, after all the times he had heard it, a line of fearful tension still rose up his back.

"Apaches," he said, spurring his horse.

Reeves followed.

They approached from the east, skirting the base of Flat Top Mountain, climbing a ridge overlooking the mouth of Little Aguja Canyon. On the plain below them, a circle of Army wagons and horses held off a wave of charges by Mescalero braves. Among the Indians, Thomas saw a figure he knew.

"That's Pretorio," Mullin said.

The Army circle was tight. Thomas felt a surge of momentary pride. He had helped train these men, and, even though most of the young ones had never seen action, they had retained their lessons. The circle, though shrinking, hadn't been breached, and Mescalero bodies littered its circumference.

As Thomas watched, Pretorio signaled, and another wave of Apaches charged the Army encampment. Mullin estimated the Mescalero force stood at a hundred and fifty.

"Our boys won't last another hour," Mullin said.

"My Lord," Reeves answered.

A hard knot had formed in Thomas's stomach. He lifted his mind away from it, and moved his horse down the slope of the canyon wall.

"What are you doing, Sir?" Reeves said.

"There's one thing that can stop this. I want you to ride back to Fort Davis and tell them what happened. Get them to fortify, and wire out for help. Lie if you have to, tell that fool Forsen the order came directly from Seavers. If we can't stop them here, they'll be at the fort tomorrow."

Reeves started to ride down after Mullin. "I'm staying with you, Sir."

"No you're not!" Thomas let his anger show. "You don't have a choice, Trooper. If it goes bad here, and you don't warn the fort, there'll be a massacre. Do you understand?"

Reeves stopped his horse. "What are you going to do?"

Mullin turned away from Reeves, continued down the slope. "What I have to."

Halfway down, the knot still tightening his gut, Thomas turned to make sure that Reeves had gone.

Once again, a surge of pride filled him to see that the trooper had done what he was told.

Slowly, Thomas rode straight down at Pretorio, until he was sure the old Mescalero had seen him. Fifty yards separated them.

Pretorio stared, sat straight on his horse, rested his hand under his throat, then suddenly threw his arm up and halted the battle.

His braves returned, riding silently to stand behind him.

Dust settled. Suddenly the battlefield, save for cries of the wounded, was silent.

Pretorio dismounted, stood regarding Thomas stonily until Thomas did the same.

The two men approached one another.

The circle of Army defense broke open. Two figures, one of them leaning on the other, who Mullin recognized as Adams and Chase, came toward him. Behind them, troopers stood, straining to see.

"Thomas!" Lieutenant Adams shouted hoarsely. "What in hell are you doing!"

Mullin looked briefly toward Adams. "It's all right, Bill."

Adams called, "Forget it! We'll whup 'em on the field!"

"Mr. Mullin!" came the unmistakable cry of Seavers. The Captain sounded barely in control. He pushed out of the ring of men in the Army camp, took a few cautious steps forward, halted. "You will cease this action immediately!"

Mullin ignored him.

Adams had stopped halfway between Thomas and Seaver. "Do what he says, Thomas!"

"You know this is the only way," Thomas said. He turned his attention to Pretorio, walked forward. The distance between them now was only twenty yards.

"I order you to desist!" Captain Seavers screamed. "You will not take this day of glory from me!"

Still locking eyes with Pretorio, Thomas said to Adams, "Better shut him up, Bill, or he'll get us all killed."

Kicking the dust in frustration, Adams turned, hobbled back toward the Army camp.

"I order—"

"Shut up, Captain," Adams said evenly.

Thomas turned briefly to see the Lieutenant knock Captain Seavers to the ground.

Inwardly, Thomas smiled.

Again, he locked stares with Pretorio.

Only ten feet separated them. Both Thomas and the Mescalero halted. Behind Pretorio, his medicine man, who Thomas recognized as Springs of Life, approached, stood a step behind.

"So, Buffalo Soldier," Pretorio said, "time has brought us together once more."

Thomas nodded. "This meeting should have happened long ago."

Pretorio's hand once more brushed at the spot under his neck. "I wish that it had."

Choosing his words carefully, Thomas said, "I only wish the great Pretorio could see that, in war, things happen which bring continuing grief. Sometimes, a grief cannot be healed, and leads to foolish action. Perhaps, without his grief, the great Pretorio would not have brought his young braves to a new war, which can only bring more grief."

Pretorio stood still as stone. Behind him, Springs of Life began to speak quickly, shaking his head. Pretorio held his hand up, silencing the medicine man.

"Your words," Pretorio said slowly, eyes locked on Thomas's, "hold much truth."

"Then meet me in challenge," Thomas replied. "Avenge your grief, but end the war. Send the young men home with their squaws, and let them tell the tale to their children that the great Pretorio was a wise man, who knew that peace was better than war, but that vengeance was still just."

Pretorio, face set in stone, slowly nodded. "It will be so," he said. He turned to Springs of Life, muttered a few words. Then he shouted back to his waiting braves.

Immediately, the braves set their weapons down, began to form a large circle around Pretorio and Thomas. Springs of Life moved back into the circle with them.

From the Army camp, Bill Adams hobbled over. He tried to push through the circle of braves but was held back.

"Thomas, isn't there any other way?" he called out.

"Just keep Seavers quiet. Tell the men not to interfere, no matter what," Thomas said.

"Damn it," Adams spat. He turned back. The troopers were filing out of the camp, keeping a discreet distance, rifles at their sides, watching.

Thomas unbuttoned his shirt, watched as Pretorio stripped down to his leggings, baring his chest.

A brave ran forward, held two knives out in his palms.

Pretorio pointed at Thomas, and the brave turned to him, letting him choose.

Thomas took one of the knives. Instantly, he disliked the feel of its handle. Pretorio took the other knife. The brave ran back, completing the circle.

Pretorio held the knife out before him, a salute.

Thomas did the same.

Pretorio nodded. "You will die, Buffalo Soldier."

Thomas said nothing. He waited for Springs of Life to make the sound, a loud humphing in his throat, which would start the fight.

The sound came.

The circle of braves erupted into cheering.

Pretorio and Thomas went into knife-fighting crouches, circling one another warily.

From the corner of his eye, Thomas saw the Army troopers coming closer to the circle to watch.

Pretorio, eyes hard as stones, made the first strike. He feinted to Thomas's middle, then swept quick as lightning at his side, making a shallow cut.

Thomas gasped, pulled back, tried to return but missed in a wide arc.

Pretorio moved quick as a cat to one side, raised his knife high and stabbed down at Thomas. Mullin blocked the strike with an arm, was forced down to his knees and then onto his back. Suddenly, Pretorio was upon him, knife pushing down against Thomas's arm. Shifting, Thomas caught the chief's wrist in his hand, pushed it back.

Lightning quick, Pretorio shifted the knife to his left hand, stabbed it down. Thomas threw himself aside and the knife struck dust.

Thomas scrabbled to his feet, turned, found Pretorio charging him. Again he went to his knees. He pushed himself back, using

Pretorio's weight, continued to move. Suddenly, he had the Mescalero on his back, one arm pinned.

Thomas held his knife to the Indian's throat.

Pretorio moved his free arm, held Thomas's wrist with an iron grip, sought to push him back. Thomas held tight, shifted his weight so that Pretorio's only leverage was with his free arm. The arm began to weaken. Slowly, the knife blade was moved back to the Indian's throat, where Thomas kept it.

"Now, you must kill me," Pretorio said.

"No."

Thomas broke contact, put his knife in Pretorio's hand and rose.

Staring hard into Thomas's eyes, Pretorio said, "I am avenged, Buffalo Soldier." Holding Thomas's knife in a hard grip, he pulled it into his chest just below his throat.

Eyes still on Thomas, a silent smile of triumph on his face, Pretorio died.

Adams broke through the disintegrating circle of braves.

"Thomas—"

"It's all right, Bill," Mullin said. "It ended the way he wanted."

Mullin straightened, watched the Apaches filing silently to their mounts. "You won't have any more trouble from the Mescaleros," he said. "Get an escort to follow them from a distance. Any closer and you'll hurt their pride. They'll keep their word. I'd recommend no action be taken against them when they get back to New Mexico." He smiled wryly. "Get Seavers to give that order. It'll make him feel useful."

Adams grinned. "I tied Seavers up."

Thomas laughed. "My God, Bill—"

A trooper ran up, saluted Adams. "Excuse me, Lieutenant Adams. Captain Seavers has broken his bonds, and requests that I put you under arrest." Behind the young man, two other troopers stood, embarrassed, rifles at ready.

Thomas laughed again. "Stockade, for sure! Don't worry, Bill, soon as I get back, I'll testify at the court-martial."

"Where you going?" Adams said.

"If you get a free moment, tell Seavers I found Senator Loggin's son. He's dead." Thomas pointed to Flat Top Mountain, looming over them beyond the mouth of Little Aguja Canyon. "The killer's up there."

"You're gonna need help, Thomas. I'll get a detachment, at least Sergeant Chase—"

Mullin shook his head. "I have to go up alone. Right now, it's the only way to get him. He's killed a lot of people, including the Pinkerton men. If I don't come back down, get word to Lincoln Reeves. A group of well-outfitted riders could try to hunt him down, but I don't think they'd be able to. This man's fast and subtle. I'm afraid he could melt into the shadows, leave this part of the country, kill a lot more people somewhere else. That's how dangerous he is."

"My God, be careful, Thomas. Even that fellow Sherlock Holmes had his Reichenbach Falls."

"I know," Mullin said. He smiled grimly. "But he got to come back to life."

"Sir?" the young trooper said to Adams, politely.

"It's all right, son," Adams said, clapping the private on the back. He held his hands out in front of him. "Lead me away." He turned back to look at Mullin, who was buttoning his shirt, gazing up at Flat Top Mountain.

"You remember," Adams said. "Be careful."

"I will," Thomas said, still gazing up at the cloud-touched summit of Flat Top Mountain.

# *Chapter Twenty-Two*

The Army of the Night was fighting for him!

This was marvelous!

He couldn't believe how well his general had served him. There must be decorations, awards. Instantly, he knew what they would be. But they would have to wait till later. Right now, he wanted to get the best possible look at the battle, a supreme leader reviewing his troops, cheering his army to victory!

He scrabbled down from the higher ledge, a few hundred feet from the summit, where he had first seen the signs of coming battle. Dots on the hillside had resolved into Indians in the lower hills, filling him with loathing until he had spotted, deep below him in the valley, the camped ground which at first puzzled, then elated him. As he climbed lower, his hopes had been fulfilled—until, a few hundred feet from the mountain's foot, on an outcropped shelf of rock, he squatted, moving his eyes from side to side, peering with intensity, until—yes! Black faces!

The Army of the Night!

The Indians moved down on his troops, and the battle was joined. He watched with fascination, feeling himself almost in a dream. Again and again the Apaches charged, but his army—*his army!*—held them back. Annihilation of the enemy would surely come—and then all other enemies would be destroyed. No mercy! The Army of the Night would be a ruthless foe, and soon all in the Sun's dominion would be brought under night's rein. Night would rule the Earth! And he would rule the night!

But then—something odd. He measured at the corner of his vision a single rider entering the canyon below. The rider looked familiar. Peering closely, he saw that it was one of his own, a soldier of the night. Black skin. At first he thought it might be his general, whom he had not been able to locate in the encampment below. But no—this was not his general. The figure was general-like, though—erect, proud, with a leader's bearing. A general of generals! Where had he seen him before? Suddenly he wanted to meet this man, to scramble down the mountain side, clap him on the back, give him courage. "Be brave," he would say, "there are many awards and medals awaiting you. You have command of my army. You are the strongest of the Army of the Night. Make me a cigarette." Then he would smile, and send his greatest general into war, and the Indians would flee like animals from a wrathful god.

But wait! He stayed where he was, watching the scene below with wonder. Already, the enemy was afraid of this man! The black rider merely rode into the canyon, dismounted his horse, and all fighting stopped! Remarkable! This truly was a man of the night, a general of generals! This, truly—

What was this! Even more wonderful! He pushed himself back from the cliff edge, twirled in a dancing circle, tittered, unable to control his happiness. Not only had the fighting stopped, but his soldier, his general, was meeting the Indian chief, calling him out for single combat! A fight to the death! What mastery! And then, after vanquishing the Indian chief, no doubt the other Apaches would be slaughtered ritually, their bones stamped to dust and mud, the first of the sun-worshippers to feel the wrath of the Army of the Night—

The fight began! Man against man. He clutched at the edge of the cliff, cocked his head, unable to take his sight from the battle below. Knives! He saw the glint of them, heard a distant shout as someone was cut. His general? Impossible! There—the fight went on, man circling man, the flash of blades, his general was down, fought back, again the circling, the Indian lunged—

Yes! His general of generals had the Indian pinned, held the blade to his throat. But what was happening? Nothing! His general would not kill! What was this outrage! His general stood up, merciful—and then, outrage of outrages! He allowed the enemy to kill himself! He saw the Indian thrust the blade into his chest, die with honor!

No, no! This was not right! His army was not a merciful one! Theirs was the realm of death and night! There could be no mercy in this realm! If it became known in the world that the Army of the Night was a merciful foe, then all would be lost! How could there be fear with mercy!

He pushed himself back from the sight, beat his fists on the ground. A cry came into his throat but he strangled it—it would not do for his army to hear him like this, or the enemy to know his displeasure. Still, perhaps there was redemption yet, perhaps even now the slaughter of the enemy, the turning of their bones to mud and dust, was happening below him—

He turned back to see—horror! This could not be! The Indians were dispersing, going to their horses and being let free! This was unimaginable! This was mercy as sacrilege, the complete opposite of his wishes!

Again he stifled a scream. Below, his general of generals, the traitor, was staring up the mountain toward him. Did his general know where he was?

Suddenly, he remembered where he had seen this man before. Blasphemer! This was the one who had dared to dig the bones from one of his graves. This was no general of generals! This was a traitor, a blasphemer who would die!

He looked down at the man staring upward.

Come up, then, for your reward!

There was only one solution. He would lead the Army of the

Night himself! He would take their lead, and make them a blight upon the land, and a measure of black fear would come into all those who saw them coming, a black covering, travelling night, the death of crops and man and animal in their wake. All those who opposed him would die, unmercifully, and their bones would become mud and the mud would dry and blow across the night, which would be eternal over the earth.

But only after this general of generals, this traitor, even now beginning the long climb up to his realm, reached the summit, and met his god, and was torn to pieces for his pleasure.

# *Chapter Twenty-Three*

Thomas found signs almost immediately. At the base of the mountain trail, he discovered an exact match for the bootprint he had cast in Limpia Canyon, along with a copy of the heel of the other boot. It was dried and baked hard, under an outcropping that had protected it from the recent hailstorm. Probably, it had been made around the same time in March when the rains had come.

Farther up, he found a shelf of rocks with signs of recent occupation. There were scuff marks everywhere, which any night's wind would have erased. Mullin went to the edge of the shelf. Below was a perfect view of the opening of Little Aguja Canyon, and the battle just concluded.

A slight chill went through Thomas.

Cautiously, he moved farther up the mountainside, a steady slope. He avoided overhangs above him. Here and there were signs of recent travel—a kicked rock, a brush of dusty dirt.

After three hours of climbing he stopped to rest. He realized that he would reach the summit around twilight—not the best time. But he had no choice—if he did not trap Curtis Marks tonight, he was sure the man would melt into the night. He would be twice as hard, if not impossible, to catch the next time.

He took a long drink from his canteen, capped it, went on with his climb.

There were other signs, now. Marked on the trail were the symbol, a circle with a cross pointing west. He found them every five hundred feet. As he got closer to the summit, the symbols proliferated, one each hundred feet, then closer and closer until they were virtually side by side.

Again a chill went through Thomas. He pictured Curtis Marks squatting, possessed, etching hundreds of these symbols that bedeviled him, a mental and physical trail up to the horror at the top of the mountain that he couldn't face.

Now, suddenly, the daylight had become dimmer, more orange.

The day was ending.

Thomas climbed the final steep steps to the summit of Flat Top Mountain. The view was breathtaking. A level plain, a hundred yards on a side, spread out like a shelf below heaven. Around him was sky, orange-blue. In the east, a fattening crescent of moon was hiking up the horizon; in the west, the sun, fatly orange, sank despondently. Overhead, a sprinkle of stars already heralded the coming night.

As Thomas had imagined, he followed the path of etched symbols over the plain of the summit toward the western edge and the dying sun.

There, near the edge, was the grave. It was larger than the others he had seen, dug and filled with consummate care. The circle looked perfectly round. At the head, facing the setting sun exactly, was a perfectly crossed line of stones, each fit precisely to its neighbor like a miniature rock wall.

Within the circle, constructed in similar fashion, lines of stones outlined the words, THE WOMAN.

Thomas wished he had a pinhole camera with him, to record the gravesite. His memory was enough for him, but he wanted others to see what he saw, to believe what he barely believed.

There was the slightest sound. Thomas broke his reverie to turn.

Eeriness descended. Behind him, the plain of the summit was clear. There were not many places to hide; there was nothing nearby. His eyes told him he was alone.

He turned back to the grave and faced Curtis Marks. The man stood a mere foot away, staring into Thomas's eyes, moving his head from side to side like a serpent. For the merest moment Thomas was afraid to his bones, remembered *The Hound of the Baskervilles,* the cries he had heard in the night, imagined Curtis Marks was supernatural, had appeared out of air in front of him.

Curtis Marks cocked his head, seemed to stare at Thomas from the side of his eyes. "You come to be punished?" he said, in a surprisingly mild voice.

Thomas said nothing.

"You could have been a great general," the young man said. He lifted a filthy hand, put it to his chapped, red-raw sunburned face. "When I saw you, I saw greatness. The leader of my Army of the Night. But instead, you sought to usurp my place . . ."

The young man let his voice trail off, shook his head sadly. He stared, head still cocked, at the ground. Then his head shot back up. Quick as a bird, he moved his head to the other side, stared at Thomas, took a step forward, pointed.

"You betrayed me!" He spun, pointed to the huge circular grave behind him. "I would have given you great trophies, bones to wear around your neck—"

"You let your mother's bones stay intact, Curtis?" Thomas said.

Marks turned, hissing. "The Woman was not my *mother.* My mother was . . . young and beautiful. Men . . . desired her. The Woman was shriveled, and sick."

"Did she beat you, Curtis?" Thomas said. "Did she hurt you, tell you you were bad—"

"She left me alone!"

In the falling purple twilight, Curtis Marks stood up on his toes, turned his head from side to side in anguish, raised his fists. "She . . . brought me home, and she . . . left me alone!

She told me I was too old to be held. But she held them, kissed them. When I was little she held me, kissed me—but then she wouldn't!"

"How old were you, Curtis?"

"Seventeen!"

"What happened when you were seventeen?"

A sob of anguish escaped the young man. "When I was sixteen we had a cake, and a party, and it was just me and her. But then, when I was seventeen, she shut me out! There was no cake. There was nothing! She said I was too old to be her boy, and she sent me out. I saw one of her men coming in as I left. He tipped his hat as he passed on the step. I didn't see his face. The night was falling, and the stars were up! I ran to the observatory, I ran to tell the man with the glasses. But the observatory was closed!"

Curtis collapsed to the ground, curled into a ball, rubbed his fisted hands into his eyes. Thomas took a step forward but the young man suddenly drew a long blade, held it out, warding Thomas off.

"Tell me what happened then, Curtis," Thomas said.

The young man wailed. "The stars! The night covered me, and I made a cigarette and watched the stars with the dome at my back. When day came, I went back. The man was just leaving. I saw his face—it was the man with the glasses, the man from the observatory!

"He was all that I had, and she took him, too! I ran into the house, and then—The Woman was there!"

"What happened, Curtis?"

Curtis uncurled, and sat on the ground, puzzled. "I ran away, then. I told them I was older. They told me to make them a cigarette. Always, make them a cigarette. So I left there, too. I went back and took her from her bed, and brought her here under the stars, my night."

"Who did you take from her bed?"

"The Woman. I never saw her face . . ."

"It was your mother, Curtis. The Woman was your mother. What did you do to her?"

The evening had purpled to black. The horizoned moon gave them bare shadows, while overhead the stars were coming into their glory, a million tiny beacons, untwinkling in the clear desert air.

Curtis Marks turned his head slowly, side to side. He seemed to be looking through Thomas.

"No . . ."

"The Woman," Thomas said slowly, "was your mother."

"No!" Once more the young man beat his fists to his eyes. He threw himself to the ground, clawing down into the edge of the circular grave with his knife blade. Thomas's hand went to rest on the handle of his sidearm. He took a cautious step back.

"She . . . no!" The young man dug deeper, dropped the knife, came up with something long, a leg or arm bone, ghostly white. "I hit her!" he shouted. "I came home and hit her!" He held the bone aloft. "In the sunlight! There was my telescope, and I hit her!" He tittered, stumbled to his feet. "The man from the observatory was gone, but I told them he did it. He went to jail, but all she did was stare at me, hiss at me, her ruined throat—"

More quickly than Thomas ever thought he would be, Curtis Marks jumped at him in the dark. Thomas didn't even get his gun out of his holster. The young man knocked him down, laughing, beating at his face with the white bone.

"I . . . will . . . rule . . . the . . . night . . . and . . . day!" Curtis Marks shouted, hitting Thomas with each word.

Thomas Mullin felt himself dropping toward unconsciousness. He felt himself being dragged. He tried to focus on the stars, saw a blur of tiny lights, double pinpoints. He flailed his hands, trying to find something to hold onto. He felt his hand drop into a shallow hole, run over something long and hard. He closed his fingers around it.

Curtis Marks tittered. Thomas felt his legs slide into nothingness up to his thighs. He shook his head mightily, sat half up, struck out with the object in his hand.

Curtis Marks cried out. Thomas's vision unblurred. He saw himself sitting on the edge of the precipice. A few feet below was a narrow rock ledge where Curtis Marks had hid himself before appearing. Below it was the void.

The young man had sunk to his knees beside him, holding the side of his head. Thomas reached out with the bone he held to strike Marks again, but the young man flailed his arms out, muffled the blow and caught Thomas in a grip.

Thomas pulled the young man toward him. As Curtis Marks rolled onto him he felt himself sliding off the precipice.

With the young man still held to him, Thomas's back hit the ledge below the precipice. The wind went half out of him. His grip loosened on the young man. His arm went out, felt nothingness mere inches away.

Thomas's vision had cleared. He saw a mantle of stars around the young man's head as Curtis rose up, holding the white bone in his hand high for a blow—

Thomas thought fleetingly of Sherlock Holmes at Reichenbach Falls. As Curtis Marks, shouting, brought his weapon down, Thomas slid hard to the inside of the ledge, throwing the weight of the young man to the outside. The blow glanced the side of Thomas's face, but the young man was unbalanced. He fell to the side, letting go of the long weapon, clutching vainly for support as he went over the side of the ledge. Momentarily, he caught the arm of Thomas's coat.

"You . . . will come too!"

The young man's vision darted up over Thomas's head. He gave a sudden gasp. His clutching fingers slipped, clawed to the edge of the cliff and then over.

"The . . . Woman!" he screamed.

Thomas rolled over to the ledge and looked down to see the young man's long fall, his face heavenward, cocked slightly to one side, filled with horror, staring upward past Thomas at the starry screen of the western night until he hit the rocks below.

Breathing heavily, Thomas rolled onto his back and lay, safe on the ledge, staring at the splendor of the sky, to see the risen bright lamp of Venus shining gloriously down upon him.

# *Chapter Twenty-Four*

Trooper Reeves was the first to meet Thomas riding back into Fort Davis. It was a beautiful late morning. A cool dry breeze from last night's exceptionally clear weather gave the desert a luster and lucid beauty it rarely held.

"You all right, Sir?" Reeves said, saluting, pulling up beside the older man and keeping pace. The fort sat a mile distant, a cluster of low buildings dominated by a Union flag flying tall above its parade ground.

"I'm fine, Lincoln," Thomas said, quietly. He gave a slight smile. "You might as well tell me all the good news, now."

"Is it that obvious, Sir?"

"You came riding out here with more than just greetings," Thomas said. "I can tell by your silly grin, and how hard you rode, that you're just bursting with something more than curiosity."

"Did you get him, Sir?" Reeves asked.

"Yes, I got him."

"Well—" Reeves began, excitedly.

"He was very interesting. I've been thinking all morning about his hate for himself. He murdered his own mother, you know. And he had a love for the stars, which he gained back in Chicago. In his ill mind, he confused the Sun with himself. As a *son,* he had beaten his mother nearly to death when he was seventeen. A loathsome act, which he dealt with by separating both himself and his mother from himself. She became The Woman to him. He became the Sun. After he brought her to Flat Top Mountain and killed her, his guilt became even worse. The age of seventeen was the dividing line for him between innocence and death. Besides killing anyone who fell on the other side of this line, he sought to kill the Sun itself. Quite interesting, Private. Or should I say, Sergeant."

Reeves was startled. "How did you know?"

"There's a place on your jacket where you already tried, without success, to sew the stripes on yourself. I suggest you let Private Rivers do it. He's good at that sort of thing."

"Sir, also—"

"Also, I've been reinstated. I am now Lieutenant Thomas Mullin again. As I was promised. The way you say *Sir,* without hesitation, or apology, tells me it's already happened. Which tells me that Seavers is no longer in command."

"Sir, please let me—"

"Is it Grierson?" Thomas said, smiling.

Reeves's face fell. "Darn it, yes, Sir." He brightened immediately. "And—"

"And Lieutenant Adams has been saved from court-martial, and Seavers's orderly Forsen has been demoted."

"I give up," Reeves said, and Thomas laughed.

They rode on silently. Finally, the young man turned to Thomas, smiling.

"What is it, Sergeant?"

Reeves said, proudly, "There was one other thing, Sir. Something you don't know about."

"Oh?"

"You got a package, from back East. I took the liberty . . ."

"And?"

"Magazines, Sir. A whole new stack of those *Strand* magazines, from England. With the Sherlock Holmes stories in them."

"Ah," Thomas said. "I suppose we're going to have to teach you to read those magazines."

Reeves smiled. "Yes, Sir. Something for me to hold tight to, Sir."

Thomas nodded, and they rode on.

General Grierson did Thomas the honor of waiting for him outside his quarters when he rode in. Grierson had gained a few years, if not pounds, but, by evidence of his still-piercing stare, long-trimmed beard and erect bearing, he still looked ready to take on any fight.

"Pleasure to see you, Sir," Thomas said, saluting.

"The pleasure is mine, Thomas. It's been a long time, and a lot of shuffled papers out East, since I've seen you. Sorry I had to come out here and clean up this mess. But from what I hear, you've been keeping your end of the Tenth Cavalry as sharp as it was since we organized it back in '67."

Thomas smiled, dismounting his horse. "We've tried, Sir."

Grierson walked forward and shook Thomas's hand warmly. "I'm sure the Sergeant here has told you all the news?"

Thomas turned his smile on Reeves. "Yes, Sir, he has."

"Senator Loggins is very grateful for what you did. We're going to have his son's remains sent back to St. Louis. If there was a trial . . ."

"There'll be no trial, Sir. Curtis Marks's body is at the foot of Flat Top Mountain. The boots he's wearing are all the physical evidence we need to prove who he was. There won't be any more killings."

"Good. You know, Thomas, they're talking about closing this post up. But I think we have a couple of years left in it. We have a lot to catch up on, later. But first, I, um, hear you have some unfinished business." Grierson turned, and Lieutenant Adams hobled out of the shadows of the porch of the officer's quarters, Forsen, looking chagrined, at his side.

Adams took Mullin's hand. "Good to see you, Thomas." He nodded toward Forsen. "Been saving him for you."

Grierson said, "Normally, I don't approve of this type of thing. But I believe Private Forsen has something to clear up with you before his transfer goes through." He walked to his office, not looking back, and closed the door behind him.

A small circle of enlisted men had gathered, leaving Thomas and Forsen in the middle.

Forsen looked at the ground. "I've got no trouble with you now."

"You did a few days ago," Thomas said. "And you forgot to call me Sir."

"That was before—Sir."

Forsen's fists suddenly came up, and Thomas saw the raw hatred in the man's eyes. "Hell, you're still a nigger," Forsen spat, "and Grierson's a nigger-lover."

Thomas blocked Forsen's punch easily, knocked the man to the ground with a solid blow to the jaw.

Forsen tried, then failed to get up.

The circle broke up. Thomas unstrapped his saddlebags from his horse, settled them over his shoulder, began to cross the parade ground to his quarters.

"Hey, Thomas!" Adams called.

Thomas turned, looked at his friend, who stood next to Sergeant Reeves.

Adams said, "Better pack! They're moving you into the main officer's quarters!"

"Later, Bill."

"Sir?" Reeves asked.

"What is it, Sergeant?"

"Can we—?"

Thomas turned back toward his quarters, motioned for Reeves to follow.

"Come on, Watson," he said, hearing the young man whoop happily and run to catch up. "You and I have some reading to catch up on."